PUBLIC SCHOOL SUPERHERO

JAMES PATTERSON

AND CHRIS TEBBETTS

ILLUSTRATED BY CORY THOMAS

SCHOLASTIC INC.

ISBN 978-0-545-91253-2

Copyright © 2015 by James Patterson. Illustrations by Cory Thomas. Middle School® is a
trademark of JBP Business, LLC. All rights reserved. Published by Scholastic Inc., 557 Broadway,
New York, NY 10012, by arrangement with Little, Brown Books for Young Readers, a division of
Hachette Book Group, Inc. SCHOLASTIC and associated logos are trademarks and/or registered
trademarks of Scholastic Inc.

12 11 10 9 8 7 6 5 4 3   17 18 19 20/0

Printed in the U.S.A.   40

First Scholastic printing, September 2015

FOR THE KIDS OF PAHOKEE,
BELLE GLADE, AND ALL
THE MUCK CITIES

—J.P.

THE REAL ME

*T*oday I, Stainlezz Steel, am officially bugged out. Today's my first day at Union Middle School, and the truth is, I'm a little scared.

Don't laugh. My school is way worse than your school. Believe that.

In real life, I am mild-mannered, easy-to-get-along-with Kenny Wright. And as you may have figured out by now, Stainlezz Steel only exists in my crazy mixed-up imagination.

Superheroes aren't real. I know that. But you show me a kid who says he never wished he could fly like Superman, or run like the Flash, or mess around inside Iron Man's supersuit...and I'll show you a kid who's lying through his grill.

That's why I made up Stainlezz Steel. Inside my head, I mean. Because I have about as much chance of being a superhero as a turtle has of winning a hundred-yard dash. And the only battles I ever win are on the chessboard.

Not like Steel.

It doesn't help that my stubborn-as-a-donkey Grandma Hope insists on walking me to school, either. (I call her G-ma for short. She calls me Kenneth, for long, but you can just call me Kenny.)

I explained to G-ma that I'm in sixth grade now. It's straight-up embarrassing to show up with your granny on the first day. Everyone thinks I'm kind of a geek to begin with. Well...maybe not a *geek-geek*, but I'm definitely not "that dude." You know that dude; the ladies love him, and the fellas want to be him. But try explaining that to G-ma. She may not be hard of hearing, but she can definitely be hard of listening, if you know what I mean. And she has an opinion about EVERYTHING.

And don't get me wrong. I've got mad respect for G-ma. She takes good care of me, and I try to do the same for her. She also makes the best peach upside-down cake you ever tasted.

It's just that I'm crazy nervous about starting middle school. Like, throw-up-on-my-shoes nervous. Kids like me can get stomped down pretty quick at a place like Union Middle.

But G-ma doesn't notice. On the real, for a little old lady, she has a lot of heart. She's fearless. Sometimes I think she may be a champion MMA prizefighter at night. Hey, it's possible. She just keeps walking on down Martin Luther King Avenue, talking to me about grades and high expectations, while I try to hold on to my breakfast and figure out how I'm going to make it through the first day.

Times like these, I could use a little less Kenny and a lot more Steel.

3

WELCOME TO UMS

Okay, in my neighborhood, my school is known as Fort Union. That's because of the crazy-strict military base rules there.

No kids get inside until 7:50 a.m., sharp.

No kids get inside without a student ID.

No kids get inside without opening their backpacks for the security guards.

And that's just the front door. I'm sure it'd take you less time to get through the airport's high-tech security with explosives tied to your calves. It's crazy, man. This is what I go through, every stinkin' day.

When I get past security, I find that my homeroom doesn't even have real windows. It's just metal screens where someone broke out the glass over the summer.

Also, it's kind of crowded in here. "Overcrowded" would be an understatement. For real.

After attendance, my homeroom teacher, Ms. Green, takes us around the school and shows us where everything is.

Downstairs on the first floor, the library's about the size of a closet. There's one rolling computer cart with two computers for the whole school. Also some wrinkly old posters of President Obama, Dr. King, and Rosa Parks on the wall. They just look sad and tired, which I don't think is supposed to be the idea. I may come in really late one night as Steel and hang up a few Malcolm X, Marcus Garvey, and Sojourner Truth posters. Yeah, like that.

Ms. Green shows us the cafeteria next. Then I ask her where the gym is, but she just shrugs.

"They've got a gym at Union High," she says. "Here at the middle school, we just sectioned off a part of the parking lot. Sometimes we take students to the park down the street."

UMS COMPUTER TECHNOLOGY CENTER

And I haven't even talked about the other kids yet.

At UMS, the sixth-grade classes are on the second floor. Seventh grade is on the third floor. And eighth grade is on the fourth floor. In other words, the higher you go, the more dangerous it gets. Because those eighth graders...I can't even front...they can be a little intimidating—scratch that, they can be straight-up scary sometimes. About half of the boys have full beards, and I've seen at least three girls with healthy mustaches. No lie.

Believe me, you do not want to get caught alone on the fourth floor in this place.

Or in the stairwell.

And definitely not in the bathroom. *Never* in the bathroom. I've already decided that if I ever have to go, I'm just going to hold it until high school. Peeing your pants is not a good look, but you know, sometimes in life, especially life at Fort Union, a brotha has to weigh his options. Carefully.

So wish me luck. I think I'm going to need it.

4

MY TINY PROBLEM

*F*irst period, I have history with Mr. Hillcoat. He comes in, writes his name on the board, and then tells us to open our books. "Start reading," he says. "Keep reading till the bell. No one will be permitted to use the restroom, and please, whatever you do, don't disturb me. Thanks, guys." Then he takes a seat at his desk, props up his muddy kicks, and watches *SportsCenter* on his iPad.

I'm pretty sure there are some good teachers at Union Middle School. Maybe even some great teachers—the kind who make everything fun and who really want you to do your best.

Mr. Hillcoat is not one of those teachers. He's a bum, or what we in DC call a bamma: a clueless, useless person. Or it could mean

someone who dresses like a clown. That's
Mr. Hillcoat. Bamma to the millionth degree.
He looks like he just stepped out of a bad film
from 1984. His gear is busted. Straight busted.

Also, my history book is so old, it *is* history.
Like maybe George Washington's kids used it
when they went to middle school. The only thing
holding it together now is some old yellow
packing tape. But I don't think Hillcoat
notices or cares.

This is another thing about UMS. There aren't always enough seats to go around. My history class has twenty-five desks and twenty-eight kids.

Actually…make that twenty-*nine* kids, because Tiny Simpkins just rolled in.

I know Tiny from around the way. He's always up to no good. He's taller than any sixth grader should be—six foot two, and just as big around. He also has four older brothers: Tommy, Terrell, Tony, and Theo.

Theo plays football, middle linebacker, for Howard University. He may even go pro if he can control his temper. Terrell and Tommy play football at Union High, and of course, Tony plays football with the eighth graders. They have anger management issues, too. The Simpkins brothers are no joke. If you see any of those guys coming your way, your best move would be to freeze, like a chameleon. And you better hope that you blend in with that mailbox or that light pole, because if they see you, it just might be curtains for you, son. For real. Man, they beat people down just for fun—for *fun*!

"Wassup, Grandma's Boy?" Tiny says. He always calls me that, which is just one of the reasons I can't stand him.

"Wassup, Tiny?" I say back.

"No, man," he says, stepping up on me. *"Wassup?"*

And then I figure it out. He doesn't mean *What's up?* He means *Get up off of that seat, or else.*

And I think—

See, kids like Tiny love to come after kids like me. I always want to say, "Man, it's not my fault I get good grades, so step off." (It's actually G-ma's fault. She makes me do *all* my homework, *all* the time.) But I figured out a long time ago that I have

a better chance of surviving all the way to college
if I do three things: keep working hard in school,
don't talk about my grades, and don't give kids like
Tiny any other reasons to beef with me.

So instead, it goes more like this—

'Cause let's face it. Unlike Stainlezz Steel, I've
got *no* chance against someone like Tiny Simpkins.
And I never will.

AMBUSHED!

*T*he fun doesn't end at 3:15, either. After the final bell, I get ambushed by G-ma.

Well, not exactly ambushed, since I knew she was coming. See, my grandmother used to be a teacher herself. She spent sixty-one years in the public schools—and if that doesn't make you tough, nothing will.

Now she's a reading tutor for kids who need it. That happens right after last period, three days a week. And *that* means I have to hang around and wait for her, one hour every Monday, Wednesday, and Friday. Just like last year at my old school, and the year before. And the year before that.

Sometimes I'll do my homework, or read a book. Sometimes my friend Arthur Wong will hang with me, like he's doing today. Arthur likes a lot of the same stuff I do. He's got an awesome comic collection, and he's just as good at chess as I am. Someday we're going to be champions and battle in the world-class tournaments.

Meanwhile, we take turns kicking each other's butts.

It may not look like it, but chess is a war. It's two armies going head-to-head, and only one of them can survive. I like to think of my pieces like the Avengers, or the Justice League. Every different piece has its own superpowers. Knights can turn invisible and sneak around corners. Bishops are made of rubber, and they can slip through anything. Queens have superstrength. That kind of stuff.

So actually, it's not so bad hanging around after school. Especially when Arthur's there.

The only problem is, you know who else is around right after school? The detention crew. The D-Squad. And they tend to be the kinds of kids I was talking about before—the ones who call me Grandma's Boy and give me quick, hard jabs to the kidneys in the hall when no one's looking. Which is most of the time, at UMS.

So I'm not that surprised to see Ray-Ray Powell come sneaking around.

Ray-Ray's not like the other bullies. He's not extra-big, or extra-strong, or even all that scary. He's just extra-annoying.

And he's always—I mean *always*—begging for food.

"What up, fellas?" he says. He already knows from fifth grade that I usually have something good for an after-school snack. So of course he's here.

Today it's G-ma's homemade chocolate chip cookies. I already gave one to Arthur, but I put them away the second I see Ray-Ray coming.

"Go away, Ray-Ray," I say. "Don't you have detention or something?"

"Not today," Ray-Ray says.

Meanwhile, Arthur moves his knight and takes one of my pawns. I don't mind. I have a game plan. I always do. In chess, you have to think as far ahead as your brain will let you.

"Why's that piece bigger than the others?" says Ray-Ray, pointing at my king.

"'Cause he's the king," I say. "Leave it be."

But Ray-Ray picks it up anyway.

"Cool," he says. "A black king. That's what's up!"

"Put it back!" I tell him, which is a mistake. The second Ray-Ray knows you care about anything, it's like he can't get enough of bugging you about it. And I think—

I reach for the king, but Ray-Ray doesn't budge. He's got my number. He knows I won't step to him.

"What you got to trade?" he says, looking at my backpack like he has X-ray vision on those cookies or something.

It's Arthur's chess set. I don't want him losing his king. So I pull out one of the cookies. "This is the last one. That's all I have," I say. Which is a lie.

Ray-Ray hands me back the king and shoves that cookie down in one bite.

"Dang," he says with his mouth full. "You got it made, Grandma's Boy. She hooks you *up*!"

"Don't call me that," I say.

"Man, stop getting all sensitive on me. You know what you are, fool."

"We done here?" I say.

Before he leaves, he wipes some crumbs off his shirt and they fall on the chessboard. "See you, Wong," he says. "See you, Grandma's Boy."

Then he rolls out of there, all high and mighty like his poop don't stink. But it most definitely does—literally. Dude is smellin' *foul*! But then I look down at his kicks and notice that he must've stepped in a heap of dog crap. Somehow, he hasn't noticed yet, and I don't say a word. It's karma, baby. If you treat people like poop, that's what you receive. A heap of it.

Doo times two.

"You know, he's just going to keep coming back,"

Arthur says. "It's like feeding a stray cat."

"Whatever," I say. I'm not afraid of Ray-Ray. "One day I'm gonna snap on that fool. You'll see." But the truth is, I'm afraid of fighting. Nobody ever showed me how, and it's not exactly the kind of thing you learn from your grandma.

"If it makes Ray-Ray go away, that's all I care about," I say.

I put my king back on the board where it belongs. Then I slide my bishop diagonally over three squares and look up at Arthur again.

"Oh, man," Arthur says.

"Checkmate," I say.

6

CLEANING UP
THE STREETS

At 4:15, I meet G-ma by the front door. She hands in her visitor pass at the security desk and we head out.

First stop, Ricky's Market, for some sausage, peppers, and onions. G-ma's making my favorite subs for dinner.

"So how was your first day, mister middle schooler?" she asks me while we're walking.

"Fine," I say.

"Excuse me? That was an essay question," she says, "not multiple choice. You can do better than that."

Here's the thing, though. I don't want G-ma worrying. The more she knows about Tiny, and

Ray-Ray, and how I don't stand up for myself, the more she's going to worry.

And the more she's going to watch over me.

And the more everyone's going to keep calling me Grandma's Boy.

And the worse it's going to be for me at school.

You see how that works?

So I just tell G-ma about my classes, and which teachers I have, and what was for lunch. That kind of stuff.

Besides, G-ma already has enough to worry about. It's just the two of us, and we don't exactly live in the best neighborhood in DC. Straight ahead, there's some shady dudes hanging out on the corner. I see them exchanging money and unidentified items in Ziploc bags so fast, they could be magicians. G-ma and I mind our own business and keep it moving.

I know she wants to tell them to take their "hustle" somewhere else, but even she keeps her mouth shut sometimes. Not for long, though. Now that she's seen Union Middle School from the inside, she's got plenty to say about *that*.

"They should take a bulldozer to that sorry

building and start from scratch," she says. "The library alone is a disgrace. And right here in our nation's capital! I'd bet you a nickel if someone told the president what was down here, he'd want to do something about it."

And I think, *Well, maybe*. It's not like Union's invisible or anything. And the White House is only 4.3 miles away from our house. I looked it up on Google Earth once.

But I don't say any of that to G-ma. I just nod my head. To be honest, my grandmother's more like a superhero than I am. Once she makes up her mind about something, you can bet more than a nickel it's going to happen.

Well...with a little help, maybe.

THE SUGAR SHACK

A week later, I get in a fight at school.

But probably not in the way you think.

First, let me tell you about the Sugar Shack. If it's coated or loaded with sugar, they've got it. That's what they call the cafeteria, because that's pretty much what everyone eats there. But it's not all sugar. No indeed. Everything else is deep-fried or comes from a box, or a lab, or something. Nothing meant for people to be eating, that's for sure. Apple slices and broccoli bites? Nahhh… you're on your own, kid.

The Sugar Shack has everything that's wrong with UMS, all in one giant room. It's totally run-down, it's crazy crowded, and it can be dangerous, if you're not careful. There's mad noise bouncing off every wall. A kid named Reverb is the resident lunch DJ. He hooks his smartphone up to two of those Beats by Dre Pill portable speakers. Every lyric being shot from those speakers is uncensored, and none of the teachers seem to mind. They just want to make it through the day without getting into it with any of the students. I don't really blame them. I'd compare the vibe of the room to…y'know, I don't even know what to compare it to. Maybe Lagos. That's in Nigeria. It's one of those megacities, with eight zillion people and the worst traffic jams in the world.

Yeah, that seems about right.

Most of the kids at UMS get free lunch, including me, which is cool. But that means the food line is always a mile long. By the time I get my lunch, there's usually about fifteen seconds left to eat it before the period's over.

And today, I don't even get that far.

I'm waiting in line with Arthur and our other friends, Dele and Vashon. We're just standing there, minding our own business and talking about if you had to choose, would you rather be Batman or Iron Man. (Iron Man, no doubt. I'm all about the flying.) Then someone yells out—

"INCOMING!"

I don't know what's coming in, but I duck anyway. Then I hear this *splat* sound. When I look up, Quaashie Williams has a mess of mashed potatoes running down his front.

I look behind me, and Quaashie Richter's standing there looking guilty as sin. Something tells me those potatoes were meant for me, Arthur, Dele, and Vashon.

"Oh, man," Vashon says. "Let's get out of here!"

See, we've got two Quaashies in our class, and the funny thing is—they can't stand each other. The whole thing's about to go nuclear, you can tell.

On the other hand, I'm finally near the head of the line. And I'm starving.

Arthur, Dele, and Vashon don't wait for me to make up my mind. They scatter. Quaashie W. comes after Quaashie R., and the next thing you know, I'm stuck—*BAM!*—right in the middle.

This is what I was talking about before. I may not be fighting, but I am most definitely *in* a fight.

Some kids start yelling. Other kids start throwing more food. It's getting out of control, fast. I can even taste blood in my mouth.

Wait—no. That's raspberry Jell-O. At least, I hope it is.

Then all of a sudden, our vice principal, Mrs. Freeman, breaks the whole thing up.

"That's enough of that!" she says. She pulls the Quaashies apart like a big grilled cheese sandwich—and I'm the cheese. Man, am I glad to see her! I think she just saved my life.

"Thanks, Mrs. F—" I start to say, but she grabs me by the arm.

"Let's go. All of you, to the office. Right now!"

"Huh?" I say.

"You heard me. MOVE!"

Before you can blink twice, she's dragging me, Quaashie, and Quaashie out of the cafeteria and up the hall.

The Quaashies are still yelling at each other. Mrs. Freeman's yelling, too. I'm trying to explain what happened, but it's like shooting a water pistol at a hurricane. Nobody really notices.

Mrs. Freeman drops us outside the principal's office, goes in, and shuts the door. And just like that, I'm in trouble. For something I didn't do.

Something I've never done in my life.

How did I get *here*?

9

TROUBLEMAKER FOR LIFE

When Mrs. Freeman comes outside again, I try to explain—again. She just tells me to take it up with Mr. Diaw.

"Who?" I say.

"The principal," she says. "Who do you think?"

I've never met Mr. Diaw before. He's brand-new this year. Union Middle School goes through principals the way the Cleveland Browns go through coaches.

But that's not what I'm stressing about. I'm wondering what Mr. Diaw is going to do when I get inside that office. I mean, I'm the victim here. This is all a big misunderstanding. I just need a chance to explain, and everything will be okay.

Right?

When the door opens, there's a short, bald

man standing there with a nasty-looking tie and
an even nastier frown. I guess that's Mr. Diaw.

"Inside," he says. "Let's go."

When we get inside the office, he has three
files out on his desk. I can see my name on one of
them: KENNETH LOUIS WRIGHT. Now I start to sweat.
Something about that file gives me a bad feeling.
That, and the way Mr. Diaw is just...staring at us.

"You know, it takes me ten seconds to size up a

student," he says. "Even less for the troublemakers. And in my book, that's what you three are. *Troublemakers*."

Then he starts to scribble something in those files. Including *my* file. I don't know what's worse—the scribbling or the staring.

"But I didn't do anything," I say. "No lie."

"Mm-hm," he says, and keeps on writing.

"Quaashie, man," I say to Quaashie W. "Tell him. I just got caught in the middle. For real!"

"It's true, Mr....um..." Quaashie says. "Wait. What was your name again?"

Mr. Diaw just looks up, shakes his head, and pulls three pink slips out of his desk drawer.

"Are those *detention slips*?" I say.

"They're not party invitations," he says.

I can hardly believe it. But Mr. Diaw isn't looking at me anymore, and he doesn't want to hear any lip. Or excuses. Or even what really happened.

"First thing after school on Friday, you three will report for detention," Mr. Diaw says.

"But—" I say.

"That's it."

"But—"

"Now get back to class!"

"But, Mr. Diaw—" I say.

"GO!" he says. "While I'm still in a good mood!"

And that's when I know I'm dead. G-ma's going to skin me alive when she finds out about this.

I mean…IF she finds out.

Which I guess means one thing. I have to make sure she never does.

Somehow.

NO-GOOD, LOW-DOWN DIRTY DOG

Mr. Diaw has me down as an official troublemaker now. That's jacked up. And G-ma's at the school three afternoons a week! Man, this is *not* going to be easy. If she hears about my detention, I'm done like Shaq's short rap career.

I guess I could try to explain. But look how that went with Mrs. Freeman and Mr. Diaw. Maybe G-ma would get it…or maybe she'd just come down on me even harder than ever. I'll be getting called Grandma's Boy for so long, they'll have to start calling me Grandma's Really Old Man.

When I get home, I go straight to my room and hide my head inside a book. It's not that hard to do. Our apartment's like a library. G-ma's got bookshelves in every room in the house. Even the bathroom—no kidding.

KENNY'S CRIB

At home, I have to read every day. That's the rule. Even Saturday and Sunday. Even Easter and Thanksgiving. Right now, I'm holding my copy of *Bud, Not Buddy* in front of me like some kind of shield. We're reading it for English, which I figure will make G-ma happy. She thinks it's one of the best books ever. In fact, I already read it last year.

"Kenneth!" G-ma says, and I almost jump out of my skin. "I called your name three times. Are you reading, or daydreaming?"

"Reading," I say.

"Just so you know, we're eating early tonight. Then we've got a neighborhood meeting," she tells me.

"Can't I stay home? Please?" I ask, even though I know the answer. I always have to go to these neighborhood meetings of hers. It's a whole lot of yakkety-yak most of the time.

"No, sir," she tells me. "In fact, I want you to say a few words tonight."

"*What?*" I say. "What kind of words?"

"About what it's like to go to that run-down school of yours. That's what the meeting's about."

G-ma's all about *words*. She likes books. She likes conversation. And as you can tell, she likes *talking*. A lot.

As for me, I'm all about saying as little as possible right now.

"I don't know, G-ma," I tell her. "You really think people care about what I have to say?"

The way she looks at me, I can feel the lecture coming on like a thunderstorm.

"Kenneth Louis Wright," she says. "Don't you think a decent education is worth speaking up for?"

"Well, yeah," I say. "But—"

"Words are our weapons against what's wrong in the world." She keeps going. "Why do you suppose Mr. Christopher Paul Curtis bothered to write that book in your hand?"

"To tell a story?" I say.

"Yes. But why?" she says.

I think about it for a second. "Because he had something to say."

Now G-ma smiles like I made her proud. It's kind of the best feeling in the world. But it doesn't last long, because then I remember that I'm also a low-down, no-good lying dog of a grandson.

"Tonight I want you to tell *your* story," G-ma says. "Everyone has one. And every story's valuable. You're old enough to understand that now."

I want to say, *I'm also old enough to stay home alone.* But instead, I quit while I'm ahead. Or at least, while I'm still alive.

"What time's the meeting?" I say.

11

YAKKETY-YAK...WHAT?

When we get to St. Anthony's Church for the meeting, there are a bunch of people there. Almost all adults. I guess G-ma's not the only one who wants to talk about school stuff.

By now, I'm freaking out about what I'm supposed to say. G-ma thinks I'm some kind of model student, but I'm sitting on this secret detention of mine. How am I supposed to "tell my story" now?

Just when everyone starts taking their seats, I decide I've got to come clean first. She always keeps it real with me. Always. It's the least I can do, you know, out of respect and everything.

"G-ma," I say. "There's something I need to tell you."

"Can it wait, Kenneth? We're about to start," she says.

"I don't think it can," I say. "See, something happened today—"

But then I get cut off. Mrs. Clark from the neighborhood stands up at the front and claps her hands to get everyone's attention.

"Thank you for being here," she says. "But I'm afraid I have an unpleasant announcement to make."

G-ma's not listening to me anymore. She's looking at Mrs. Clark.

"What is it now?" G-ma mumbles.

My heart's going fast and furious—yeah, just like the movies, but not so cool, and no Vin Diesel or pretty girls standing around in short-shorts. Just me with a pair of clammy, sweaty palms and an embarrassing case of cotton mouth. I know. Weak, right? I just want to bounce.

"G-ma," I whisper. "It's not my fault, but today I got a—"

But Mrs. Clark keeps talking. "We just received word that Principal Diaw will be leaving Union Middle School, effective immediately."

WHAT? I think.

"WHAT?" G-ma says.

"Mr. Diaw has been transferred to a different school outside the district," Mrs. Clark says—and then everyone starts talking at once.

I don't really hear a lot of it. Mostly I just hear the parts about "Mr. Diaw" and "leaving."

And I'm pretty sure they won't be getting around to me anytime soon. No more story to tell! I'm off the hook! Well…at least for now.

I know this isn't good news for the school. It's exactly the kind of thing that makes G-ma so mad about UMS.

Everyone in the room, G-ma included, is growling, fussing, and straight flippin' out. So I just stay in my seat with my mouth shut and a serious mean-mug drawn on my face.

But on the inside, it's a little more like this—

LIFE ON THE D-SQUAD

*I*t doesn't take long for me to figure out that this is more like *half* a piece of good news. With Mr. Diaw gone, it gives me a fresh start at school—but I still have that stupid detention to worry about. By the time last period ends on Friday, I'm crazy nervous all over again.

Still, I have an idea. And Arthur's going to help.

Right after school, G-ma shows up to do her tutoring like always. I meet her by the front door and get my half-healthy, half-junk-food after-school snack. She gives me a banana and then some kid gives me a pack of Oreos because he says he's allergic to that creme stuff in the middle. Weird alien kid, right? I mean, who's allergic to that classic cookie nectar?

G-ma goes off to the library and I say I'll see her in an hour.

So far, so good.

I run by the classroom where Arthur and I usually play chess. He's got the board set up and ready to go, just in case. I give him half of my banana and two Oreos. Then I head over to the detention room down the hall.

When I walk in, I see Quaashie, Quaashie, Ray-Ray, and a few other kids. They're all on the D-Squad today. Just like me.

"What you doin' in here, Grandma's Boy?" Ray-Ray says. "You take a wrong turn at the water fountain?"

I ignore Ray-Ray and sit on the other side of the room. Then Mrs. Freeman tells us all to pipe down and get to work. Fine with me.

For about ten minutes, nothing happens. I'm still mad about being here in the first place, but at least G-ma doesn't have to know.

Except then...I hear it. Someone's whistling out in the hall. Darth Vader's theme from *Star Wars*. That's the signal Arthur and I set up.

When I look over, he's standing there staring at me. He puts two fingers up to his eyes, points them back at me, and then looks up the hall toward the library.

Code red! G-ma's looking for me!

"Mrs. Freeman?" I say. "I have to go to the bathroom."

She just looks at me like that's the most tired thing she's ever heard. "You can wait," she says.

"I don't think I can," I say. Then I ball up my fists and cram them in my lap like I'm stopping up a leak. A stupid, messy leak. Then I make the most painful-looking wince, like the Hoover Dam is about to burst and flood the valley.

"I got to go, too!" Ray-Ray says.

"Yeah, me too!" Quaashie R. says.

Then Mrs. Freeman surprises me. "Kenny, you can go," she says. "The rest of you I don't believe."

That's probably going to earn me a couple of jabs to the kidneys later, but I can't worry about that right now. I take a hall pass from Mrs. F. and bounce.

Arthur's eyes look like two big moons when I get to him. I think he's kind of afraid of G-ma.

"I told her you were in the bathroom," he whispers. "I think she believed me, but—"

But whatever. I'm already running up the hall. I've got to make this quick.

When I get to the library, G-ma's got a bunch of kids sitting around a big table. "Oh, Kenneth, good," she says. "Vanessa here has forgotten her copy of *Bud, Not Buddy*. May we borrow yours, please?"

More bad news! See, that book's sitting in my backpack. And my backpack's hanging on a chair in the detention room. If I go back in there now, that's it. Mrs. Freeman's going to lock me down tight for the rest of the hour.

And I think—if Steel was here, this would be no problem.

Of course, Steel *isn't* here. It's just me. And I've got to think quick.

"I'll be right back," I tell G-ma. I walk out of the library, but as soon as I hit the hall again, I'm running like Whiplash is coming after me with ten million volts.

The good news is Arthur has a copy of *Bud, Not Buddy* in his locker. The bad news is Mrs. Freeman must think I'm taking the world's longest pee. By the time I deliver that book to G-ma and sprint back to the detention room, Mrs. F. is standing in the door waiting for me.

"What took you so long?" she says. "I trusted you, Kenny. And why are you out of breath? Running in the halls isn't allowed. I ought to give you another detention."

She lets me slide, though, and I head back to my desk.

Maybe I should be relieved, but I'm not. All I can do now is sit here pretending to do my homework and waiting for my heart to stop doing backflips inside my chest.

Is this what a life of crime feels like?

Because those knuckleheads can have it. For real.

GET READY FOR DR. YETTY

On Monday morning, G-ma walks with me to school again. She wants to meet the new principal, somebody named Dr. Yetty James.

I know that "Dr." doesn't have to mean like "stick out your tongue and say ahh," or "you only have fourteen hours to live." But still, I'm wondering if this new principal's going to be good news, bad news, or something in between.

When we get to school, there's a lady out front saying good morning to everybody. She's tall, and has this huge smile, and she's even really pretty. I'm talking Beyoncé/Alicia Keys/Rihanna pretty. Like that.

G-ma walks right up to her and says, "Dr. James, I presume?"

"Everyone calls me Dr. Yetty," the lady says, and shakes G-ma's hand. "And whom do I have the pleasure of meeting here?"

"I'm Kenny Wright," I say.

"And what are you good at, Kenny?" she asks me.

I'm not really sure how to answer that one. It seems like a weird question, but G-ma answers for me.

"He's an excellent student," she says. "And he's quite the chess player, too."

"Ah, a kindred spirit," Dr. Yetty says. Whatever that means. "We'll have to play sometime."

"*You* play chess?" I ask her. I don't mean it to be rude, but G-ma shoots me a look that says otherwise.

"Kenneth, you go on inside," she tells me. "Dr. Yetty, if you have a moment, I'd like to chat a little."

And I think, *Uh-oh!* This is exactly what I was afraid of. G-ma's been waiting all weekend to fill the new principal's ear. It also puts her one step closer to finding out whatever Mr. Diaw wrote in my file before he left.

"G-ma, Dr. Yetty's just getting started," I say. "Maybe you should cut her some slack and talk later."

"Nonsense," Dr. Yetty says. "What better way to start than by getting to know the people in the community?"

G-ma smiles back at her like Dr. Yetty just won the Miss Black USA contest, or invented electricity, or something. So I slide on out of there, but even while I'm walking away, I can hear G-ma starting to ask questions.

In other words, this whole new-principal thing is starting off exactly the way I was afraid it might: Sometimes even the beautiful ones bring you the most heartache and trouble. I can feel it in my big toe. It tingles sometimes when trouble is about to pop off.

And it's tingling.

A TIGHT SPOT

Speaking of trouble...

A few days later, I get my next beat-down from Tiny Simpkins. He's stepping to me pretty much all the time now, but some days are worse than others.

Like today, for instance.

There I am, standing in front of my locker, minding my own, when I hear these voices behind me.

"I don't know, young. Looks kind of tight."

"Nah, man. He's got it. No doubt."

When I turn around, Tiny's standing there with his boy Jerome Cleary. His brother Tony is there, too. Tony's in eighth grade, and he looks a lot like Tiny, if you added a couple of inches and twenty pounds of muscle wrapped in blubber.

"Wassup, Grandma's Boy?" Tiny says.

"Wassup?" I say, like always.

"See, we got this bet going on," Tiny tells me. "My big brother here thinks there's no way you can fit inside that locker. But I say he's wrong."

I try to get in chill mode, but on the inside I'm already hitting the panic button. Big-time. I probably *could* fit inside that locker if someone really wanted me to.

And I think someone does.

I start to close the door real quick, but Tiny's already there to stop me.

"Hold on," he says.

"Come on, Tiny," I say. There's no use pretending anymore. "Why don't you just keep it moving, man? For real."

"'Keep it moving'?" he says. "Listen to this bamma. How about I 'move' this upside your head?"

THIS ONE IS CUSTOM FITTED JUST FOR YOU.

KENNY

Before I can do anything, he's picking me up like a human gym bag and stuffing me inside that locker. He gives me a punch in the chest, too, and then slams the locker closed. When I try to stop him, all it gets me is a faceful of door. My nose is smushed, my teeth are rattled, and my pride feels like the bottom of the boots of a guy whose job it is to clean up dog poop at the park. Yeah, like that.

Meanwhile, Tiny and his boys are wilding out in the hall. I can even see little pieces of them through the holes in the metal.

Then I hear Tiny say, "What're you looking at, Wong? You want some of this?"

They start chasing Arthur down the hall, and that's it. I'm all on my own here. There's no handle inside this locker, and nobody bothering to help me, either.

What I could really use right now is some Steel.

Or maybe a crowbar and a little oxygen tank.

My fear of cramped, tiny spaces that smell like sweaty shorts and stale socks is starting to get to me. This is jacked up.

DID SOMEONE SAY "STEEL"?

NOT NOW, RAY-RAY!

Meanwhile, back in my locker, nothing's happening. I can see people walking by, but nobody stops. Nobody even lifts a finger.

"Hello?" I say again. "Hello? I know y'all hear me. Dang…"

Then the door opens and Arthur's standing there.

"Let's go eat," he says.

That's it. Arthur knows what it's like. The last thing you want to do after something like this is talk about it. So we just head on down to the Sugar Shack and find a couple of seats.

I'm not hungry, so I skip the line. Arthur busts out his chess set and the lunch he brought from home. His dad's a porter at some fancy Chinese restaurant. Today, he's got doggie-bag chicken and an egg roll he breaks in half for me, but I don't want that, either. I just want to get this day over with.

So when Ray-Ray Powell and his girlfriend Preemie come sniffing around, I am seriously *not* in the mood.

"What up, y'all?" Ray-Ray says.

I just ignore him. Arthur does, too.

"You deaf?" Preemie says. She's the only white girl at our school, and probably one of the shortest, too. I have no idea why she hangs with Ray-Ray. She just does. She's from Chevy Chase, one of the whitest parts of the Maryland/DC area, and her pops was a crazy-rich lawyer. They fell on hard times somehow and her parents got divorced, and now her mom sells shoes at the mall. Sometimes it goes down like that.

"You can keep moving, Ray-Ray," I tell him. "We don't have anything for you to eat, all right?"

"You sure about that?" Ray-Ray says, and steps in.

I can see it coming a mile away. He's going to try and take another hostage, so I put my arms over the chessboard to stop him.

But there's too many pieces to protect. Ray-Ray snakes his own skinny arm in there and pulls a white bishop and a knight off Arthur's home row. Then he steps back, grinning like a fool.

Now, if I was Stainlezz Steel, we all know what would happen next. Ray-Ray would be straight molly-whopped.

But I'm not Steel. I'm just me. And to be honest, I'm getting pretty tired of being me. I'm up to *there* with Ray-Ray, and Tiny, and the Quaashies, and detention, and all of it.

So maybe that's why I snap—like a one-eyed man with a busted telescope.

"You want something to eat?" I say. "Eat this!"

Then I pick up that half an egg roll and wing it right at Ray-Ray's head. Some of it gets on his shirt, but most of it goes on the floor. (I don't have a rocket for an arm. You'll never mistake me for RGIII.)

Ray-Ray looks at me like he can't believe it. So do Arthur and Preemie. Even I can't believe it.

"Ohh, boyyy—shouldn'ta done that," Preemie's saying. She's got her hand over her mouth, and her eyes are all lit up like she can't wait for whatever's going to happen next.

I've never seen Ray-Ray really mad before. My heart's thumping like an 808 bass drum. So I throw my hands up to block anything coming my way.

When he comes in swinging, I jump out of the way. But it's not me he's after. It's the chessboard. His arm sweeps the whole thing off the table and everything goes flying—the pieces, the board, my backpack, and Arthur's lunch.

It makes a big noise, and it even quiets down the cafeteria—for about three seconds. Everyone looks like they're expecting a fight. But then they see it's just me and they go back to their business.

Everyone except for Dr. Yetty. She comes out of nowhere and swoops down on our table.

"What is the meaning of this display?" she says, looking all heated.

"Kenny threw food at me!" Ray-Ray yells.

"He took our chess pieces," Arthur says.

"Ray-Ray didn't do nothing," Preemie's saying. "Ray-Ray didn't do *nothing*, Dr. Y."

But Dr. Yetty isn't listening to Preemie. She's staring at me, and then at Ray-Ray, and then at me again. It's like sitting under a heat lamp, the way she looks at us.

"Both of you—Raymond and Kenneth. Clean up this mess. And then I want you to report straight to the office, toot sweet!" she says.

I don't know what *toot sweet* means, but it can't be good. Before all this, I'd never been sent to the principal's office for anything. Now I'm two for two and the school year's just getting going.

I'm starting to think maybe this place is bad luck. No, scratch that. I *know* it's bad luck.

FRIDAY THE 13TH

FRIDAY 13

BREAKING A MIRROR

GOING ANYWHERE NEAR UNION MIDDLE SCHOOL

BLACK CAT CROSSING YOUR PATH

WALKING UNDER A LADDER

DR. YETTY'S REALLY BIG, REALLY TERRIBLE IDEA

D r. Yetty has the office set up all different than Mr. Diaw did. The desk is against the wall, and there's a round table with some chairs in the middle of the room. She's also drinking coffee out of this huge mug with Muhammad Ali's picture. On the side, it says, *"Float like a butterfly, sting like a bee."*

Yeah, that seems about right.

Here comes the sting.

"Can someone please tell me what happened?" Dr. Yetty says.

"Kenny in a bad mood today," Ray-Ray says.

"Kenny *is* in a bad mood," Dr. Yetty corrects him.

"That too," Ray-Ray says. "'Cause someone put him in his locker this morning."

And I think, *How does he know that?* I guess he must have seen it, but still. I don't like Ray-Ray getting inside my head.

"I'm sorry, Dr. Yetty," I say. "I just kind of snapped."

"Don't tell me," she says. "Tell Raymond."

I get it over with quick. "Sorry, Ray-Ray," I say.

"It's cool. It's cool," he says really fast. "Sorry I messed with your game like that."

I know he doesn't mean it, though. Nobody fronts more than Ray-Ray Powell. His middle name should be Scam. He's a full-time faker.

"Okay then," Dr. Yetty says. She's looking at our files now. "Ray-Ray, you've already had two detentions this year. And Kenny, you've had one as well. Not off to a very good start, are we?"

"Dr. Yetty, I can't have another detention in my file," I say. "You've met my grandma. She's going to kill me. I'm not even kidding."

Dr. Y. nods and looks at me. Then she sits back and thinks for a minute. I can't tell which way this is going, so I hold my breath.

Just before I'm ready to pass out, she finally starts talking again. "All right," she says, "I have a proposal. Kenny, I want you to teach Raymond how to play chess. And Raymond, I want you to learn."

And I'm like—

At first, I think Dr. Y.'s messing with me. I even laugh a little, but she's not smiling. She's dead serious. The only one who's smiling is Ray-Ray.

He's all ear-to-ear with it, like he actually likes this idea.

"I'm down with that," he says, and Dr. Y. looks at me again.

"Do I have a choice?" I ask.

"Yes," she says.

"Good. Because—"

"You can take a one-day suspension instead," she tells me.

And now I'm more like—

I can hardly believe it. Dr. Yetty is even stricter than Mr. Diaw was. She's stricter than G-ma, too, and I totally didn't think that was possible. I'm not even sure what G-ma would do if I got suspended. All I know is, I don't want to find out.

"How long do we have to do this?" I say.

"Until Raymond can finish one game of chess against me—win, lose, or draw, but without asking for any help," Dr. Yetty says. "And you both have to stay out of trouble in the meantime, or I *will* suspend you. Is that going to be a problem?"

"No, ma'am," I say right away. Ray-Ray just shrugs.

And whether I like it or not, that's the end of that.

Or just the beginning, depending on how you look at it.

18

LESSON #1

The next day's Friday, which is one of G-ma's tutoring days. It's also my first chess lesson with Ray-Ray.

Ray-Ray shows up on time. Not for the chess, but for whatever G-ma brought me to eat. Dude is always hungry.

"What is that? Cake?" he says, looking at the little bag in my hand.

"Nope. It's a sack full of moldy jockstraps, mousetraps, and angry scorpions. Stick your hand in and get you some," I tell him, looking straight serious. I don't even open the bag.

"Don't even trip with me, fool," he says. "I'm not the one who threw that egg roll."

"Yeah, well, you're also not the one who has to teach *you* chess," I say. "Let's just get this over with."

We sit down and I start showing him where everything goes at the beginning of the game. Then I show him how all the different pieces move around the board—rook, knight, bishop, king, queen, and pawns.

"Dang, we're gonna be here a long time," Ray-Ray says. "Where'd you learn all this, anyway?"

"From my dad," I say. Which is true. "He's a cop. A detective, actually. He puts bad guys away for a living."

"Yeah, right," Ray-Ray says. "Why don't I ever see him on the block?"

"'Cause he doesn't live here anymore," I say. Which is also true. Or at least, kind of true.

"Good thing," Ray-Ray says. "'Cause my brother plays for the other side. You know—the one that's winning? Your pops don't stand a chance against my man Nicky."

"Whatever," I say. "Just shut up and pay attention, okay?"

After a while, Dr. Yetty comes in to check on us.

"What have you learned so far?" she asks Ray-Ray.

"This little man here is the king," Ray-Ray says, and points at the queen.

"Not quite," she says. "That's the queen, but she *is* the most powerful piece on the board."

Ray-Ray looks at her like maybe she's lying. "Since when?" he says. "The whole game's all about the king, right? Everyone works for him. No disrespect, Dr. Yetty, but *that's* power."

I'm kind of surprised, to tell the truth. Most of Ray-Ray's classes are with the learning-disabled kids. But if I'm completely honest, he seems sharp enough. I don't even know why he's in those classes.

A little later, G-ma comes strolling in, too. When I look at the clock, it's 4:20. I was supposed to meet her out front five minutes ago. How'd *that* happen?

"What do we have here?" G-ma says. "And who's this?"

I can't lie to G-ma in front of Dr. Yetty. That's as good as getting busted.

But before I can figure out what to say, Dr. Y. speaks up.

"Kenneth is teaching Raymond how to play chess," she says. "I asked the two of them if they wanted to give it a try, and they both said yes."

It's not exactly a lie, but still—I can't believe

it. Did Dr. Yetty just cover for me? She's not only smart, and strict, and Beyoncé-fine, but she's clever, too. Good lookin' out, Dr. Yetty!

"Well, isn't that wonderful?" G-ma says. "I've been trying to get Kenneth more involved. Now he's gone and done it on his own." She bends down and gives me a kiss, which couldn't be more embarrassing, but that's not what I'm worried about right now.

I'm worried about the way Ray-Ray's looking at me. He heard me in Dr. Yetty's office yesterday. He knows this is supposed to be a secret. Even though Dr. Y. just helped me out, it doesn't mean anything if Ray-Ray snitches on me.

But for some reason, Ray-Ray doesn't say a word. I don't know why, but he covers for me, too.

So I open up that piece of cake, break it in half, and slide one half over to him.

"Mmm, good cake," he says, giving that fake smile of his up at G-ma.

Ray-Ray Powell is smarter than I thought. He knows exactly how to get what he wants.

And now that he knows my secret, too, something tells me I'm in bigger trouble than ever.

It sucks when someone has something, anything, hanging over you. It's like they own you.

Sucks.

19

NOT GETTING IT

Monday, Ray-Ray's not in school, so I don't have to teach his beggin' behind anything. Then Tuesday at lunch I'm sitting there with Arthur, Dele, and Vashon, and guess who comes over and sits right down with us?

"What do you want, Ray-Ray?" Vashon says.

"I'm just sitting," Ray-Ray says. "Why do I got to want something?" He even has his own lunch tray. So then what's he doing here?

It doesn't matter, though, because I can see Tiny and Jerome coming this way. Something tells me they're going to want our table, and I'm not in the mood for another beat-down.

"Let's just go, you guys," I say, and start sucking down the last of my chocolate milk.

"Why? What's up?" Arthur says. He's got his

back turned, so he can't see Tiny coming up on us like a Mack truck.

But then the weirdest thing of all happens.

"Wassup, Tiny?" Ray-Ray says.

"Wassup?" Tiny says. He doesn't even look at me. He and Jerome just keep on walking. A second later, I hear them somewhere behind me.

"Hey, ladies. We need this table. *Now.*"

I turn around and some other sixth graders are scrambling to get out of the way. Some of them move faster than others.

When I turn back again, Ray-Ray's just sitting there, grinning away.

"You don't have to worry about Tiny no more," he says.

"What are you talking about?" I say. "Why not?"

"I told him about your pops. I made it good, too. I told him even my brother Nicky don't mess with Kenny Wright."

"What about your dad?" Dele asks me.

"Nothing," I say. That's another whole can of worms I don't want to get into.

"Is your brother really Nicky Powell?" Vashon asks Ray-Ray.

"The one and only," Ray-Ray says. And even though I've never heard of Nicky Powell, I can tell that Dele and Vashon have. All of a sudden, they're looking at Ray-Ray a little different. Nobody tells him to get up anymore, either.

Meanwhile, I'm sitting there thinking, *What just happened here?* It's like Ray-Ray wants to be... friends...or something.

And I don't get it.

What's the deal?

RAY-RAY, PREEMIE, QUAASHIE, VANESSA, AND...ME?

After school, I'm walking home when I hear Ray-Ray's voice behind me.

I turn around and he's coming up the sidewalk with Preemie, Quaashie W., and that girl Vanessa from G-ma's tutoring group.

"Where you going?" Ray-Ray asks me.

"Home," I say.

"We're hitting the corner store for some hot chips. Preemie says she never had any," Ray-Ray says.

"They're good," I tell Preemie. I don't stop walking, though. I don't really know what I'm supposed to do right now. Quaashie and Vanessa are bringing up the rear, and all of a sudden, there I am, sandwiched between Ray-Ray and Preemie.

On the real...a brotha is uncomfortable.

"What's going on?" I say. "Why're you doing this?"

"Doing what?" Ray-Ray says. "We're just hanging out. You keep on walking if you want to."

I'm six blocks from home. On the days G-ma doesn't tutor, she expects me there by 3:45 unless I tell her something else. It's never worth being late. She just makes me read more, or do the dishes, or something.

Still, I figure I can stop for a minute. If someone's hooking me up with free hot chips, who am I to turn them down? Then I'll head on home after that.

When we get to the store, Vanessa goes inside, but Ray-Ray stops on the sidewalk.

"Hold up," he says. "We're just going to hang here a second."

"What's going on?" I ask Ray-Ray.

"Nothing," he says. "We're just getting some hot—man, shut up and just chill for a second."

"I am," I say, "but why—"

Almost right away, the door to the store opens back up, and Vanessa comes flying out of there like her butt's on fire. I can see she's got a big bag of chips in her hand. And I can see some lady inside coming after her, too.

"Run!" is all Vanessa says.

I get it now, but it's too late to do anything about it. So I take off as fast as I can, just like all the others.

But I'm also thinking—

FIVE ON THE RUN

There's no way I'm stopping now. Why should I? This doesn't have anything to do with me.

Luckily, the lady from the store isn't very fast, because neither am I. I'm chugging up Minnesota Avenue behind Preemie and Ray-Ray, who are behind Vanessa, who's behind Quaashie, who's faster than all of us. He gets around the corner, and across Good Hope Road, then up between two apartment buildings, and straight onto Sixteenth until we get to W Street.

By the time I catch up to them all, I'm about ready to throw up a lung.

"Why'd you do that?" I say to Vanessa.

She looks at me like I'm super-lame. "You buying next time?" she says.

The truth is, I have a couple of dollars in my pocket, but I don't say anything. I just shake my head. This felt like it could've easily been one of those "wrong place, wrong time" kinds of moments that G-ma lectures me about.

"Dang, this is good," Preemie says. She throws a handful of hot chips in her mouth, and her eyes begin to water in seconds. That girl is crazy. She fans her tongue and then chomps on a few more like nothing ever happened. Ray-Ray passes the bag over to me.

"No thanks," I say.

"Go on," he says. "I owe you."

I guess he means for all those after-school snacks. But even so, I probably shouldn't take it. I know what G-ma would say.

I'M SOOOOO DISAPPOINTED IN YOU, KENNETH.

Still, Ray-Ray and the rest of them are all staring at me, so I take one and shove it in my mouth. They're mad hot, and they stain your fingertips for a day or two with an angry shade of red. But we love 'em.

Meanwhile, a bus is pulling up at the corner and Ray-Ray's looking like he's ready to take off. "There's my ride," he says. "You wanna have some fun?"

I don't even know what he means. None of the others are going for it, so I just stay put. Next thing I know, the bus is pulling away from the curb and Ray-Ray's running after it. He jumps up on the back bumper, grabs hold of a little grip that's hiding there, and waves at us while that bus takes him right back the way we just came.

I'm not saying it doesn't look fun, because it kind of does. Fun—but dumber than that dude in your math class who sits in the back, picks his nose, and eats his boogers when he thinks no one is watching. But you caught him one day, and all he could do was flash that goofy booger-eating grin. You know the dude.

G-ma would ground me for life if she ever caught me doing something as stupid as bus-surfing, or whatever Ray-Ray calls it.

And speaking of G-ma, it's almost 3:45. I've got to get home—now!

ACTION!

Call me paranoid if you want, but I scrub that bright-red chip residue from my fingers at a filthy gas station restroom before I even get home. You never know with G-ma.

When I get there, she's all fired up about something else, though. She's got her gospel music playing from an old radio sitting on top of the fridge. Her favorite group's some old guys called the Mighty Clouds of Joy. She's tappety-tapping away at her laptop, seated at the kitchen table. There's a bunch of papers stacked in front of her, with lists of names and I don't know what else. She even tells me to get my own snack.

"What's going on, G-ma?" I say.

"We're starting an action," she says. "Myself, Dr. Yetty, and some folks from the neighborhood."

"What's that mean?" I ask her. "What kind of action?"

"An organized, peaceful—but forceful—march for better schools, for *all* the children in our city. Not just the lucky ones. Or the rich ones. Or the ones who live west of the river."

"So, G-ma—why do this now? Why do we have to march and make signs and all that stuff? And why is Dr. Yetty getting mixed up with this?" I wonder aloud.

My G-ma could inspire a herd of gazelles to organize and rise up against a pride of lions. "The truth is, I haven't seen her kind of passion, especially from a woman so young, since I marched in Selma, way back when," she tells me.

"What I mean is, isn't she a part of what you—I mean we—are marching against? The people in charge?" It just seems weird to me to have her down with us. As far as we know, she's going to be in and out like the rest of those bammas.

"No, baby. Not at all. I love what she stands for, and so does almost every other parent. But there've been a handful of parents claiming that she pays too much attention to the male students.

Can you believe that? Some people don't like the all-boy mentoring program she started in her first week on the job. God knows that's what you boys need, but who am I?" She shrugs and then closes her laptop.

I guess G-ma has a point about Dr. Yetty. I mean, she did bring three new staff people along with her. First there's Mr. Anthony, her right-hand man. He's like a real serious administration-type dude. Then there's Mr. Yarborough, the new head of security, who's actually pretty cool. He's one of those ex–Navy SEALs, but you couldn't tell by looking at him. And there's a man who grew up right around the corner from our house, Mr. Griddine. He's what's called a Director of Strategic Plans or something. I don't know what any of those guys really do. I don't. But you know what's cool? They look like me. They look like Ray-Ray. They look like us and they're in charge of stuff. They wear suits and tell people what to do. That's something I've never seen at my school.

The way G-ma's going, I can tell we're going to be talking about this for a while. Which is fine with me. Anything right now is better than *How was your day?* or any of those other "essay questions" she usually asks. I can just see how *that* would go.

So I get busy making a peanut butter and banana sandwich while G-ma keeps on talking.

"We're going to march up Martin Luther King Avenue," she says, "and have a big rally right in front of your school."

"Cool," I say.

"I'm hoping for a thousand people, maybe more. Parents, teachers, and most of all, students—"

"Uh-huh," I say.

"Which is why I want *you* to be one of our speakers. I think you'd make an excellent student ambassador, Kenneth."

This time, I don't say anything at all, because that peanut butter just got stuck in my throat like a ball of cement.

"I know it's a little scary," G-ma tells me. "But it's no different than what I asked you to do at the neighborhood meeting."

"You just said it was going to be a thousand people!" I say.

"That's just more ears," she says.

"Well…uh…I don't think I'd make a very good ambassador, either," I say.

"Nonsense!" she says. "If we see something wrong in the world, it's up to us—not someone else—to stand up and be heard."

That's another one of G-ma's greatest hits, if you hadn't noticed. She always says you're supposed to speak up if you see something wrong.

You know—like if someone steals stuff from a corner store.

Or gets detention and lies about it.

Or has to teach chess for all the wrong reasons.

Stuff like that.

And guess what else I realize? Ray-Ray Powell isn't the big faker around here anymore.

I am.

23

STEEL VS. STEAL

24

EGYPT IS IN AFRICA

Dr. Yetty's got a special assembly the next morning. It's part of the history unit she's teaching, called "The Cradle of Civilization." That's just one thing Dr. Yetty's been doing different at UMS. She's the principal, but she's also teaching some. We call her the History Channel now. And today's assembly is all about Egypt.

"I thought this was about Africa," Ray-Ray says.

"Fool, Egypt is in Africa," I tell him.

He just shakes his head like he feels sorry for me. "You should try not looking so smart once in a while," he says. "Just sayin'."

"Yeah, well..." I mumble as we shuffle into the auditorium.

I don't sit with Ray-Ray, though. He hangs in the back, where it can get a little dangerous if you're not careful. So I find Arthur, Dele, and Vashon, and we sit somewhere in the middle, close enough to see, but far enough away to not stand out too much.

Dr. Yetty shows a whole bunch of pictures and maps and stuff. It's actually kind of interesting, and a lot of the kids are into it. She tells us that lots of important parts of things like medicine, astronomy, law, art, and music pretty much all started in Egypt.

"Which is in Africa," she keeps saying. "That's part of African heritage, too. A lot of what we see from ancient Greece originally came from Egypt..." she says, and puts a hand up to her ear.

"Which is in Africa!" a bunch of people say back.

"The Europeans, as well. They got a lot of what they're famous for from Egypt..."

"Which is in Africa!" everyone says. They're all kind of cheering and getting into it now. Why not? It's one reason to walk a little taller, and I'm all for that. Dr. Yetty is pretty amazing at getting everyone into it, so nobody feels like they're acting weird.

Check it out:

25

LESSON #2

At our next chess lesson, Ray-Ray does exactly what I expect him to do. He comes on strong and attacks, attacks, attacks. It doesn't matter to him if he gets my knight and I take his queen. He just likes the battles.

"You've got to figure out how to survive," I tell him. "The idea is to try and take something without losing anything."

"Huh?" He looks at me like I just spoke in Swahili, or the way I look at G-ma when she drops one of her old Negro spiritual quotes or African proverbs on me.

"If you can take something for nothing, that's better than having to trade, right?" I say.

Now Ray-Ray sits back and looks at the board again like he hadn't thought of it that way.

"Yeah," he says. "I can see that."

It doesn't really do anything, though. On the next move, he leaves himself wide open just to get one of my pawns. I slide in there for a checkmate, and we have to start all over again.

"Hey," he says when we're setting up the board, "long as we're talking, you want some free advice of your own?"

"Not really," I say.

"Stop walking around like you're afraid of people," he says. "It's so obvious, man."

"Yeah, yeah, okay. Thanks," I say. This is the last thing I want to talk about with Ray-Ray. But it turns out he's like G-ma that way. Sometimes it doesn't matter if you want to talk about something or not.

So he keeps going.

"You look at someone like Tiny," he says. "You can just see it in his eyes. He's not here to get knocked over. But with you and those geeks you hang out with—"

"Shut up about my friends," I say.

"I'm just saying, it's like you're carrying around a sign or something. Says, 'I won't fight back, so

go ahead and slap the snot out of me.' You know?
You're like one of these pawns, just waiting to get
picked off."

"Yeah, well, thanks for the advice," I say. "It's
your move."

Then Ray-Ray takes his bishop and tries to scoot
it around the corner like it's a knight. And I think,
This is never going to be over, is it? The way things
are going so far, I'm going to be sitting here with
Ray-Ray...forever.

Maybe longer.

"A" IS FOR IDIOTS

At first, I'm thinking there's no good reason to take advice from Ray-Ray. Why should I?

Except then…a few days later, I get this big fat A on my report for *Bud, Not Buddy*. And if you're wondering how that's linked to Ray-Ray—peep this.

When Ms. Green hands back the reports that day, she skips right past me. She holds on to my paper and goes to the front of the class.

"Pay attention, everyone. I'd like to read some of what Kenny wrote," Ms. Green says.

No problem, right? WRONG! This is just about the last thing a "Grandma's Boy" like me needs.

Arthur flashes me a thumbs-up, and Lucinda Morehead sits up a little straighter. But behind me, I can hear people making sounds like air coming out of a leaky tire. I don't have the nerve to turn around, but it feels like I've got a whole row of lasers pointed at the back of my head.

I'm not even sure which part she reads. I'm too busy waiting for it to be over. Finally, after about eight years, Ms. Green stops and asks, "Does anyone have any questions for Kenny?"

"Yeah," someone whispers behind me. "What's it like to be the world's biggest geek?"

"Are we supposed to call you Teacher's Boy now?" someone else says.

And then, "Do your legs get cold when you wear a dress in the winter?"

That one cracks everyone up, until Ms. Green yells at them to be quiet.

"Dwayne! Kwame! Quaashie!" she says. "That's enough. I'll see all three of you after class."

I know Ms. Green thinks she's doing the right thing, but I sure wish she hadn't said anything. Even though they're the ones getting in trouble, something tells me *I'm* the one who's going to pay.

I also wish G-ma hadn't made me read that book a second time. Then maybe I could have gotten a nice, ordinary B, and all those guys could have used someone else for target practice.

But you know me. I want a lot of things I can't have.

CLIMB TO THE BOTTOM

Don't get me wrong, okay? It's not like I *want* bad grades. There's plenty of reasons why As are worth working for. I get it, I really do.

But now that I'm in middle school, it's kind of complicated. See, if you're not careful, or even if you're unlucky (like if a teacher makes the whole class listen to your stupid report), then all that work can start to turn against you.

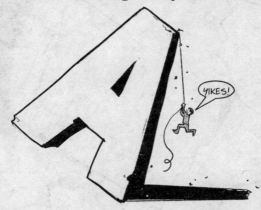

One second, you're doing okay, and the next...

That A you *thought* you wanted turns right around and bites you in the butt. And usually by then, it's too late to do anything about it.

That's how it went with my book report, anyway. Ms. Green's English class was only the *first* bad thing to happen to me that day.

The first....but not the worst.

Just wait. There's more.

28

ALL WET

After English, I make a quick pit stop in the second-floor bathroom. Which turns out to be a big mistake. Remember when I said you never want to get caught alone in the bathroom at UMS?

You don't.

But you know how it is. Sometimes, when you've gotta go, you've gotta go.

I try to make it fast. I don't even bother washing my hands (not that there's any soap or paper towels left, anyway). Still, before I can get to the door, it swings open, and in walk Dwayne, Kwame, and Quaashie R. Also known as *Crush*, *Kill*, and *Destroy*. Sometimes they even tag the outside of the building with a "CKD." Graffiti is like an art form around here, or just a way to let everybody know who's running the school.

You didn't think Tiny Simpkins was my only problem, did you? I wish! This is one way that middle school *is* like superhero comics. Every time you get rid of one bad guy, there's at least one more waiting to take his place. That's how it works. Just ask Batman. Or Spider-Man. Or Stainlezz Steel.

Meanwhile, I'm trying to get to the door, but I've got this Quaashie-sized wall in my way.

"Waddup, Grandma's Boy?" he says. "Thanks for getting us in trouble back there."

"I didn't get you in trouble," I say.

"That's not how I see it," Dwayne says. He brushes right past me and turns on one of the sinks. I reach for the door again, but then Kwame grabs my backpack and spins me right around.

That's when Dwayne sticks his thumb over the faucet. It sends a jet stream right at me with perfect aim. And I mean, right at the front of my pants. Now I look like a kindergartener who isn't quite potty trained, or a dude with a bad bladder problem. Either way, it ain't a good look.

My backpack hits the floor. Dwayne, Kwame, and Quaashie start cracking up and pointing at

me. And I'm standing there in a puddle like I need my diaper changed.

"Why don't you write about *that* next time?" Dwayne says. He kicks my stuff toward the toilet stalls, and then the three of them laugh themselves right out of the bathroom.

I don't go after them. Obviously. Even if I had the guts, I don't have the muscle. And even if I had the muscle, there's no way I'm going to go running out there looking like this.

Now I'll have to spend the rest of the day with my jacket tied around my waist, and carrying my books all front and center until I dry off. All because of one stupid book report.

I don't get it. It's not like I'm the biggest brain. I'm not a butt-kisser like Lucinda Morehead, either. And I know for a fact that some of the other kids live with their grandmas—including Quaashie R. So how come I'm the official school punching bag?

Weirdly enough, that's when I start thinking about Ray-Ray. He's even skinnier than I am. He's hyper as one of those elementary school shorties. And he's totally annoying. But people don't ride him the way they do me.

Even when someone does mess with Ray-Ray,
it's like he doesn't even care. Like nothing ever
bothers him. And I'm thinking, *How does he pull
that off? What's his secret?*

On the real—*I wish I was more like that.*

Which is the weirdest thought of all.

I mean, if you'd told me at the beginning of
the school year that I'd ever want to be anything
like Ray-Ray Powell, I'd have said you were crazy.

Straight bananas. Nuttier than one of G-ma's pecan pies, with extra nuts.

But guess what I'm figuring out real quick? Middle school's crazy, too. And *nutty* isn't always the same thing as *wrong*. Sometimes in life, you have to get in where you fit in. We just went over this in science. It's called adaptation. If your environment changes, guess what? You better change, or else.

So now here I am, actually wanting something from Ray-Ray, if I can get it. And like it or not, there's only one way to find out.

I'm going to have to ask.

NEVER THOUGHT
I'D SEE THE DAY

I wait until we're playing chess the next day, so we're good and alone. I don't want any witnesses for this.

We're about halfway into our first game. Ray-Ray's trying to figure out his next move. I even left my rook wide open on purpose, but he doesn't see it.

"I need to ask you something," I say. "But don't get all excited about it, okay?"

"How come?" he says. He's already excited. The thing with Ray-Ray is, he's kind of like a blender with no off switch. There's just fast, faster, and fastest. He probably ought to be on one of those prescriptions, but I don't think Ray-Ray gets to the doctor too much. His teeth are messed up, too.

Jacked. Looks like he chews rocks for breakfast. Every morning.

"You know how you're always saying I shouldn't let people mess with me?" I say.

"Yeah?" Ray-Ray says. "What about it?"

"Well, don't let this go to your head, but I was sort of wondering if you could maybe…you know. Tell me how," I say.

Ray-Ray just shrugs. "It's like you expect it to go down, and it shows. Looking scared's the same thing as being scared. You got it?"

"If I got it, I wouldn't be asking you," I say. How am I supposed to just *not* be scared of someone bigger than me? It's not like I can turn it off and on, or run down to the corner store for some guts.

That's when Ray-Ray starts to get some kind of new idea. I can see it on his face, like he just won a hundred bucks on a scratch-off ticket.

"So that's how we're gonna do it? You give me lessons, I give you lessons? That's the new routine, bamma?" he says.

"Who said anything about lessons?" I say. "Just tell me what to do."

"Yeah, right." He sits back and points at the chessboard. "'Cause you're just gonna *tell me* how to play chess, huh?"

I'm starting to think this was a bad idea. Not because Ray-Ray's wrong. But because he's *right*. If I'm going to toughen up, I'm going to need some kind of practice.

"I know exactly where to start, too," Ray-Ray says. Already, he's pulling out this phone I didn't even know he had, and he starts tapping away.

"Hang on," I say. "What are you doing?"

"You'll see. It's a surprise," he tells me.

And speaking of surprises, he leans in then and slides his queen all the way across the board to take out my rook.

"Bet you didn't think I saw that, did you?" he says.

Nope. I definitely didn't.

But then again, it seems like there's a lot of things I don't see coming these days.

MEETING THE KING

*J*ust before 4:15, Ray-Ray starts putting the
chess stuff away.

"Come on," he says. "It's almost time."

"Time for what?" I say.

He doesn't wait for me, though. He just walks
right out of the room and leaves me standing there.
Part of me thinks I should let him go. You never
know what's going to happen next with Ray-Ray,
and I don't mean that in a good way.

But I'm curious, too. And I did ask for his help.
So I pack up the rest of the chess stuff and head
out after him.

When I get into the hall, Ray-Ray's right there.

"What are you doing?" I say.

"Waiting," he says.

A second later, the detention room door opens,

and the D-Squad for that day comes pouring out, like the Nationals on opening day. I see Dwayne, and Vanessa, and Jerome and Tiny, too.

"I don't want any trouble, Ray-Ray," I say.

"Ain't gonna be any," he says. "Just the opposite. You remember I said how you're always acting like one of those pawns, just waiting to get picked off?"

"Yeah?"

"Well, get ready to meet the king," he says. "Watch and learn, son."

Then he starts moving again, heading up the hall just ahead of everyone else.

When we get outside, there's this black Jeep sitting out front. The stereo is *knockin'*! It's a track from Wale's first album. I can feel the bass in my chest all the way from the curb. The Jeep's right in the place where you're not supposed to park, and it's got two bad-looking dudes in the front seat. The one on the passenger side looks a little bit like Ray-Ray.

"What's good, Nick?!" Ray-Ray yells out, and keeps walking toward them.

That's when I figure out who "the king" is. It's Nicky Powell. *The* Nicky Powell. I can still remember the way Dele and Vashon bugged out when they found out Nicky was Ray-Ray's brother.

Which of course makes me even more nervous. What's someone like me supposed to say to someone like that?

Nicky looks me up and down when we get over to the car. Then he turns the stereo down, but I can still feel the *whoomp-whoomp-whoomp-whoomp* vibrating in my ears.

"This is Kenny," Ray-Ray says. He's standing on one foot and kind of bouncing up and down. It's this weird habit of his.

"Chill, Ray-Ray," Nicky says, and Ray-Ray puts his other foot down. You can tell he thinks Nicky's "that dude," because Ray-Ray never does anything anyone tells him.

"You the one who's teaching Ray-Ray chess?" Nicky says in a slow, cool drawl. He sounds like one of those late-night radio DJs, but cooler. I wish I had that voice.

"Yeah," I say. At least I know how to answer that one.

"Thanks, man. I owe you." Nicky reaches out the window and gives me a pound. "Hop in. My man Trayvon can give you a ride," he says.

The guy behind the wheel hasn't looked at me once. I don't know if that's a good thing or a bad thing. But I do know what G-ma would have to say about all this.

"That's okay," I say. "It's not that far, and my grandma likes me to walk straight home."

Nicky looks at me now, the same way Ray-Ray does sometimes. Like I'm some kind of charity case.

"We're working on it," Ray-Ray tells him. "Yo, Kenny, you've got an audience. You want to hang here with them, or you want to roll with us?"

I start to turn around and look, but Ray-Ray puts a hand on my neck.

"Just pretend they're not there," he says. "Like you couldn't care less—got it?"

I got it, all right. I just figured out that Ray-Ray's doing me a world-class solid here— introducing me to Nicky Powell, right in front of the D-Squad. I'll bet this is frying Tiny's brain into a crisp like cheap bacon. You know, the kind that shrivels all the way down until it looks like a stick of gum.

And either way, he's right. The last thing I want right now is to get left alone with that crew. So when Ray-Ray opens the car door, I go ahead and get in behind him. Then Trayvon pulls away from the curb, fast and loud. Wale spits the second verse

of the track that I can't remember the name of but
that will come back to me sometime later today.

I never look back. Not even once.

But I sure do want to.

SWEATIN' WITH THE BIG DOGS

About five seconds later, I start to wonder if I've just made a huge mistake.

This is definitely not the kind of thing a Grandma's Boy would do. But is that a good thing…or not?

"I don't live very far," I tell Trayvon. "It's just up on—"

"Sit tight," Nicky says. "We're going to make a quick stop first."

What the what!?! Now even my sweat's starting to sweat. Quick stop? What exactly is that supposed to mean?

Or do I even want to know?

The whole time we're driving, Nicky doesn't look back at us once. Trayvon hasn't said a word, either.

Before I know it, Trayvon screeches up to the curb, and Nicky hops out with his hands in his pockets. "Hold it down, Tray. This won't take but a minute," he says.

I look up at the storefront—and we're outside Ben's Chili Bowl, a DC institution. They make, by far, THE best chili dogs this side of the universe. No lie. Forget about those wannabe dogs that your mother just slops together. These babies are like heaven...in a bun...covered in chili and onions.

After about twenty minutes, Nicky comes back out with a sack full of chili cheese dogs, maybe a dozen, plus chili fries and milk shakes. Milk shakes, man!

Nicky hands Trayvon the sack. He cracks a smile and then says, "That's what I'm talkin' about. A brotha is hungry!" So I guess he can talk, after all.

When Nicky passes us a couple of straws and our milk shakes in the backseat, he looks at me kind of funny.

"What's the matter, Chess Man?" he says. "You expecting we were going to rob a bank or something?"

"Nah," I say, real quick. I laugh, too, but it comes out wrong—kind of like a goat. I'm trying to act like I hang out with dudes like them all the time, but mostly I'm just coming off as lame. A real bamma.

I figure Ray-Ray's going to make fun of me, too, but he's got his big mouth stuffed with chili dogs. Trayvon doesn't even look back and tosses two chili dogs in my lap. There aren't any fries left. Ray-Ray already took all those, but I'm not going to complain. For one thing, G-ma hardly ever lets me eat this stuff, and for another—I'M STILL ALIVE. I'd call that two for two.

As soon as we're back on the block, I tell Trayvon he can let me out on the corner. "I'll just walk the rest of the way," I say. I'm done taking chances for the day.

"Congratulations," Ray-Ray says, looking at me on the sidewalk.

"For what?" I say.

Whatever he says back, I don't even hear it. Trayvon peels out and the smell of burnt rubber fills my nose. The speakers are knocking that new Rick Ross joint. I can hear it blocks away.

But I guess I just finished my first lesson.

32

ONE THING OR ANOTHER

I'm not even late by the time I get home. But I am in trouble.

Kind of.

When I open the door, there's a whole apartmentful of people inside. I see Dele's and Vashon's moms, and a bunch of other parents from the school. Even Dr. Yetty's here, looking at something with serious eyes glued to her Kindle Fire—the latest version, of course, in a fancy-looking red leather case. That's Dr. Yetty.

"Kenny!" she says when she sees me. "How are the chess lessons coming along?"

"Uhh…fine?" I say. It seems like a complicated question, even though it's not. Half my brain is still back there in Trayvon's ride.

"When can I expect to play a game against Ray-Ray?" Dr. Yetty asks me.

"Soon, I hope," I say. Because that's no lie. Meanwhile, I'm wondering if I still have chili and onions on my breath, and if anyone saw me getting out of that Jeep.

All I want to do now is get to my bedroom and close the door, so I keep moving. I scoot around Dele's mom, squeeze past some lady on a cell phone, and get about two more steps before—

"Look who it is!" G-ma says.

She's sitting in the living room with a bunch of other people. Mrs. Clark is there, too, standing by a big pad on an easel, with a black marker in her hand. The pad says stuff like "Save Our Schools" and "Education First."

So I guess this whole big *action* thing of G-ma's really is happening. Which isn't great news for me. Because I know what's coming next.

"So, Kenny," Mrs. Clark says, "your grandma tells us you might be willing to stand up and speak at our rally. Have you given it any more thought?"

Talk about a complicated question! I look over at the door to my room, and it might as well be on the other side of the galaxy by now.

So I open my mouth, and I give the one answer that's going to get me there a little faster.

"Sure," I say. "I'll do it."

I mean, what else am I going to say?

Everyone in the living room starts clapping for me then. The people in the kitchen lean over to see what's going on, and G-ma says, "Ladies and gentlemen, meet our new student ambassador!" Now those people start clapping, too, and the whole apartment's cheering for me like I'm some kind of perfect model student. Or even some kind of superhero.

What could I possibly say to change things at our school? Why would anyone listen to what's on my mind? Maybe they'll care. Maybe they won't. I'm leaning more toward won't. It's not like I'm Marcus Garvey or Medgar Evers. If G-ma could hear my thoughts, she'd say, "No, you're not Garvey or Evers. You're Wright, and that's all you need to be."

But you know what? None of that matters. I'm still bugged out. And that's when my head just about spins right off.

Actually—no. Not that. More like it splits in two.

33
BACK AT THE LAB...

34

STARFISH

Later that night, I'm about to hit the sack when G-ma comes into my room.

"Did you feel pressured to say yes to that speech?" she asks me. "I didn't mean for it to happen that way."

"It's okay, G-ma," I tell her.

"Well, I'm proud of you," she says.

"You shouldn't be," I say.

G-ma looks at me all squinty, the way she does sometimes. "Why not?" she says.

"Well…" I shrug at her. "I haven't given the speech yet. Maybe I'll still chicken out."

"I doubt that," G-ma says. "You're a brave boy, Kenneth. You're the bravest boy I've ever known."

I can't even touch that one. No way.

"Do you really think it will make any difference,

though?" I ask her instead. "I'm just…me, you know? I don't really see how—"

"Kenneth." She cuts me off, and I already know what she's going to say. "Have I ever told you the story about the starfish?"

"Yeah," I say. She's told me that one about a thousand times, but it never stops her. I don't mind, either. I kind of like it. So she sits down on the bed and keeps talking.

"There was a young man once," G-ma says. "And he came onto a beach that was covered in starfish."

THEY'D BEEN WASHED ASHORE, YOU SEE.
THROWN RIGHT OUT OF THE OCEAN, BY THE HUNDREDS.
THOUSANDS! ALL UP AND DOWN THE BEACH FOR MILES.

"WHAT ARE YOU DOING?"

"I'M THROWING THEM BACK," THE OLD WOMAN SAID. AND SHE FLUNG ANOTHER INTO THE WATER.

THEN OUR FRIEND LOOKED UP THE BEACH. HE LOOKED DOWN THE BEACH.

ALL HE COULD SEE FOR MILES WAS OCEAN, AND SAND, AND ENDLESS STARFISH.

"ARE YOU CRAZY?" HE SAID. "YOU COULD BE HERE FOR DAYS AND NOT EVEN MAKE A DENT IN ALL THIS. WHAT DIFFERENCE CAN IT POSSIBLY MAKE?"

AT THAT, THE STRANGER PAUSED, LONG ENOUGH TO PICK UP ONE MORE STARFISH. SHE SMILED AT THE YOUNG MAN, AND THEN SHE SAID—

CHICKENS WITH FINGERS!

I don't know if I'm ready for another one of Ray-Ray's "lessons" or not, but a few days later, I get one anyway.

We're in the cafeteria at lunch, and Ray-Ray straight-up dares me to steal some chicken fingers off the steam table. I don't even like chicken fingers. Since when do chickens have fingers? Something just ain't right about that.

"Are you crazy?" I say.

"Yeah," he says, grinning that Ray-Ray grin of his. "But this ain't about me."

This is about *me*, and we both know it. I didn't exactly ace that car ride with Nicky. When you end up sweating like a pig and laughing like a goat, you're not exactly a shining example of swag.

Still, you're probably thinking, *No way*, right?

Why would I take a stupid dare like that?

Good question. I just wish I had a good answer. Maybe it's because Preemie, Quaashie W., and Vanessa are watching. (Especially Vanessa.)

Maybe it's because I still have something to prove, and Ray-Ray's never going to stop pestering me until I do.

Or maybe it's because I'm a big fat idiot.

All of the above, I guess. Whatever the reason is, the next thing I know, I'm sneaking past the lunch line…

...checking to make sure no one's looking...

...grabbing a tub of chicken fingers with a side of hot honey mustard...

…and getting out of there as fast as I can go.

Ray-Ray's right there, and we book it out into the hall. I don't stop running until we're all the way around the corner and into the stairwell, where it's quiet.

Then we get rid of the evidence faster than you can say GULP. It's like those chicken fingers just disappear.

But not for long. My stomach's already feeling kind of funky, and I'm starting to think there's more than one reason why this was a bad idea.

"Good job," Ray-Ray says with his mouth full.

"To tell you the truth, I didn't think you had it in you."

And then, all at once, I *don't* have it in me. Every bite of every chicken finger I just sucked down comes right back up. All over the stairs. All over the floor. And all over my shoes, too.

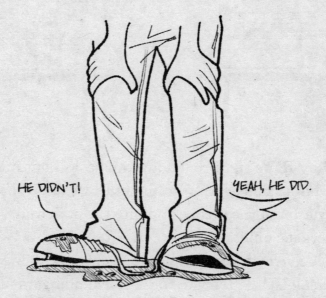

HE DIDN'T!

YEAH, HE DID.

Ray-Ray thinks it's hilarious. "Way to go, man," he says. "You're a regular gangsta now." He's loving this, I can tell.

I'm glad someone is. Because to tell you the truth, I don't know *what* I'm doing anymore.

36

MY NEW REP

I know I should stop. But I don't.

That week we have a field trip to the Smithsonian's National Air and Space Museum. I get on the bus with Ray-Ray and Preemie, partly because they ask me to, and partly because I want to.

Arthur looks at me funny when I say I'll catch up with him later. He watches me move on back, and then I don't know what he does, because I'm not paying attention to him anymore. I'm noticing how Dwayne and Kwame are looking at me.

Before this, they always looked at me like I was a cockroach they couldn't wait to stomp. But ever since they saw me rolling out with Nicky Powell, it's more like I'm some kind of puzzle they can't figure out.

And do I like it? You know it! As far as they know, I'm one of Nicky's boys. Yeah, right.

"Did you check Dwayne and Kwame back there?" Ray-Ray asks me when I sit down.

"Actually, yeah," I say. I look over again, and this time Kwame looks away first. That *never* happens. Up to now, the only people who looked away from me first were pretty girls. Well, not all of them. I catch a few cute ones giving me "the eye." Okay... maybe one or two. But I haven't developed my mack, my conversation with girls, just yet, so I look away. I know—weak!

Back to Kwame. Dude actually *looked away*.

Crazy, right?

"Now we've got to keep it going," Ray-Ray says.

"What's that mean?" I say.

"You've got the new rep, but it's not worth much if you can't back it up. People need to see you standing up for yourself once in a while," Ray-Ray says. "Even if it's not for real."

"Huh?" I say, but he and Preemie are just cheesing at each other like they've got some kind of secret plan. Which I guess they do. You never know what Ray-Ray's up to.

"It'll be like one of those pop quizzes," Preemie says to me. "So just be ready."

And I'm thinking, *Since when is Preemie in on this?*

And then I'm thinking, *What does she mean? Be ready for WHAT?*

But mostly, I'm thinking about how Kwame looked away first, and how much I like *not* being a cockroach.

So I don't ask any more questions. I just keep my mouth shut and go with the flow.

Which turns out to be a huge mistake.

AIN'T NO FUTURE IN YOUR FRONTIN'

*T*he front of the Air and Space Museum is the coolest thing I've ever seen. They have all kinds of aircraft hanging over the lobby like huge models. Except these are the real deal. I'm looking up at an old fighter jet, and a space capsule, and a hang glider, and I'm wishing I could just take one of them out for a test flight. Like maybe *now*, because Ray-Ray and Preemie have me feeling just a little bit nervous.

You know, like the way the ocean is just *a little bit* watery.

Dr. Yetty's already been working with us on a unit from the museum. It's called "Black Wings," all about African American pioneers in aviation.

So when we pass by a picture of Bernard Harris, you *know* she points it right out.

"There he is, boys and girls. The first African American to walk in space. And there's one of my personal heroes, Bessie Coleman. She was the first licensed black pilot, all the way back in 1921. Who can tell me how many years ago that was?"

That's Dr. Yetty for real—'cause why just do history when you can do math at the same time? No wonder G-ma's totally in love with her.

Meanwhile, we're all headed toward the planetarium, and everyone's pushing and jostling, trying to get there first for the good seats. Ray-Ray's right in front of me now, but I'm not sure what happened to Preemie. She was here a second ago.

And then I hear her voice.

"Ready?" she whispers behind me.

Before I can say *Yes*, *No*, or *Ready for what?*, she puts her hands on my back and gives me a push.

I stumble right into Ray-Ray. He stumbles, too, and then whips around, giving me this evil eye I've never seen on him before.

"What's wrong with you, Grandma's Boy?" he says.

I know it's not for real. Lots of other kids are around, including Dwayne and Tiny, which I guess is the whole point. This is my chance to fake-show what I'm fake-made-of. But that doesn't stop my heart from running like one of those jet engines.

Then Ray-Ray steps up on me, even closer.

"I said...what's wrong with you, *Grandma's Boy*?" he says again. He keeps his voice low, so none of the teachers notice—but everyone else does.

And here's the part I don't expect. Even though it's fake, I still hate that name. All of a sudden, I'm thinking about everyone who ever called me that.

Everyone who tripped me in the hall, or stuck me in a locker, or pounded me like Bryce Harper does to every ball pitched his way.

And that's when I start to get mad. For real.

"Check yourself, Ray-Ray," I say.

"Check myself? You better get back in your lane, before I put you there," he says. I can tell he's trying not to laugh. He looks over at Jerome Cleary, standing there watching us. Tiny, too. "And what're you gonna do about it, Grandma's B—"

Before I know what's what, I reach out and give Ray-Ray a shove. It's nothing I was planning on. It just kind of happens. I don't think Ray-Ray was expecting it, either. He looks pretty surprised when I do it.

Then he looks even more surprised when he falls over one of those fancy ropes they use to keep us in line.

The security guard looks surprised, too. Especially when Ray-Ray falls right into her.

And she drops her walkie-talkie.

And it makes this huge *SQUAWK* sound when it hits the ground.

And a bunch of other guards come running to see what's going on.

The good news is, I just passed Ray-Ray's pop quiz. But that's the only good news. Next thing I know, Dr. Yetty's putting a death grip on my arm and dragging me away.

"What kind of display was that?" she says. "I'm shocked, Kenny. Shocked! I think your grandmother will be, too."

My heart never even slows down. That fight may have been fake, but the trouble I'm about to get into is one hundred percent real.

Plus, G-ma's going to be *two* hundred percent disappointed. I can just see her face now. Letting her down kills me. I'm supposed to be some type of student ambassador dude. You think Frederick Douglass got into fake fights?

No way.

That little silver-haired lady is gonna let me have it.

She's like a living, breathing, pint-sized civil rights movement.

G-MA GOES OFF

WHAT WERE YOU THINKING?"

That's one of G-ma's favorite things to say. But I've never heard it quite like this. She already got the scoop from Dr. Yetty. But now that I'm home, she wants to hear it from me.

And she's not just *kind of* mad. She's not even *really* mad. This time, G-ma's got it turned all the way up. That's the kind of power that can be used for good *and* evil. You haven't seen angry until you've seen my grandma heated.

"Since when does my grandson get into fights?" G-ma says. "I don't even know who you are anymore."

"Well—" I say.

"And at the Smithsonian Museum, of all places? Honestly, Kenneth!"

I'm trying to think of a way to explain this
that won't make G-ma madder—like that's even
possible.

Not to mention, she's still talking.

"This is about your *future*," she says. "That
doesn't start tomorrow, or next year. It starts today,
Kenneth. *Every day.* If you wanted a shot at a
perfect record, it's gone now. Do you hear what I'm
saying?"

And that's the part that makes it even worse.

G-ma thinks this is my first detention. She thinks this is the first time I've gotten in trouble, period.

She even thinks the only reason I'm teaching chess to Ray-Ray is because I'm some kind of good person.

Wrong. Wronger. Wrongest.

I can't keep holding it all in. I've got to tell her at least a little bit of the truth, or my brain's going to explode right here and now.

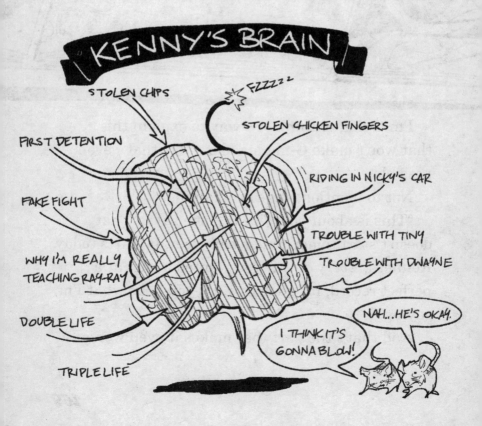

"G-ma, can I say something?" I ask her.

She bunches up her mouth and squints at me, so I can see she's taking her time to think about it.

"You may," she says then. "Help me understand this, Kenneth."

"The truth is, I thought if some of the guys saw me cutting up, they might not think I was such a... um...you know..."

I freeze, because I was about to say *Grandma's Boy*. That would be like pouring gasoline on a fire. And then jumping into the fire.

"Such a what?" she asks me.

"Um...a poot-butt." G-ma gives me a look. "I mean, an easy mark, G-ma," I say. "It wasn't even a real fight. We were just messing around, and I guess it got out of hand."

It feels good to tell her all that instead of another lie. But it doesn't get me very far. She's already pacing around the kitchen again.

"Well, until you can learn *not* to let things get out of hand, you're grounded, mister," she says.

I don't even try to argue. There's no such thing as winning an argument with G-ma. Talking about it just makes you lose slower.

And then, just when I think it's over, she says, "Except for the chess."

"Excuse me?" I say.

"That's the one thing you may continue to do," G-ma says. "I'd hate to disappoint that nice young man. What was his name, Raymond?"

"Ray-Ray," I say.

"Yes, well, there's no reason he needs to suffer because you can't behave," G-ma says.

"But—"

"You're going to see those lessons through, and that's that!" G-ma says. Then she walks right out of the room.

Just before my brain goes...BOOM!

TOLD YOU SO.

I HATE WHEN YOU'RE RIGHT.

SOME KIND OF MISTAKE

41

YOU TOO?

The next day, I ask Arthur if he wants to play chess at lunch, and he's like, "Whatever."

Arthur *always* wants to play. He's crazier about chess than I am. So I know something's up right away. And I'm pretty sure it's about Ray-Ray.

"What's up with you, man? Is it about what went down at the museum?" I say. "Or is it because we haven't had a good match in a minute?"

He just shrugs, but at least he's setting up the board. Dele and Vashon are there, too, and they're both looking at me like I just stepped out of a flying saucer with three eyeballs plastered on my forehead, and a butt where my nose should be, plus…I stink. Real alien funk, man.

"What?" I say. "Ray-Ray? It's not like we've been hanging out a lot. I just told Dr. Yetty I'd teach—"

"Ray-Ray, yeah. You already said," Vashon tells me. "Don't worry about it, Kenny. It's a free world."

So I go with the same vibe they're throwing. "Okay, whatever," I say, and start setting up my pieces on the home row.

"Why do you even want to hang with him, anyway?" Dele asks me after a couple of moves.

I don't know what to say to that. These guys know about why I'm teaching Ray-Ray, but I haven't told them anything about what he's teaching me. I mean, what am I going to say—that I'm getting anti-wimp lessons? He's showing me how not to be a Grandma's Boy?

Yeah, *that's* not too embarrassing.

It's like some other kind of chess, where the pieces are secrets and I'm playing as hard as I can to protect the most important ones. So far, though, all it's gotten me is a bunch of ticked-off people. (And one exploded brain.)

"Anyway," I tell everyone, "Ray-Ray's not so bad, once you get to know him. He's not nearly as annoying as I thought."

"Oh, yeah?" Vashon says, and points to the other side of the cafeteria.

When I turn around, Ray-Ray's sliding this girl's whole lunch tray off her table while she's tying her shoe. He spots me watching him, gives me a nod, and disappears into the Sugar Shack crowd.

"Seems pretty annoying to me," Arthur says.

"Well, we're going to be done with the chess soon," I say. "Promise."

Dele and Vashon aren't even listening anymore, and Arthur just castles his king without saying anything.

I'm starting to feel about as popular as day-old meat loaf around here. So I don't stick around.

"I'll catch y'all later," I say.

"Whatever," Arthur says.

The one other thing I do before I leave the cafeteria is stop at that girl's table.

"Here," I say. "You can have my sandwich."

I think her name's Rosa. She looks up at me like she's going to cry, and to tell you the truth, that's the last thing I want to deal with right now. So I drop the sandwich on the table and keep going.

By the time I leave the cafeteria, I feel like the scum that scum wipes off its own shoes at the end of the day. At least I know what my next move is.

WHAT'S UP WITH THAT?

"Why'd you have to take that girl's lunch?" I say when I hook up with Ray-Ray for chess that day.

"I was hungry," he says. Like that explains everything.

"It wasn't cool at all, man," I say.

"Why not? I did it to you," he says.

"Yeah, and look where it got me," I say.

Ray-Ray laughs like that's a good one. Then he reaches over and breaks off half the brownie on my side of the table.

"You know what, Ray-Ray?" I say. "I don't want to do those other lessons anymore. I quit."

"Serious?" he says. "What's the deal? We still good, right? Me and you?" The way he talks and chews that brownie at the same time, it looks like he's got a mouth full of mud.

"It's messing me up. I'm *maaaaad* grounded. And it's, like, the opposite of good. Being cooped up in the house is a bad look. I can't afford to keep getting in trouble."

"What about the trouble you've been getting *out* of?" he says. "When was the last time anyone stuck you in a locker?"

"Well—" I say.

"Or jabbed you in the kidneys? Tied your shoelaces together? Slapped a 'kick me' sign on your back?"

"I don't know—"

"Or called you Grandma's Boy? Or swiped your chair? Or knocked down your—"

"Okay, okay," I say. "I get it. I'm a walking target."

"Wrong," Ray-Ray says. "You *were* a walking target." Then he sits back and puts his hands behind his head like he's Donald Trump, with chocolate-covered teeth, and minus the swamp-rat-looking hairpiece.

"So maybe Ray-Ray knows what he's doing," he says.

"Well, I hope so," Dr. Yetty says. She just

appeared out of nowhere. Maybe she's a mutant or a magician or something. Dang!

I just about jump out of my kicks. I'm wondering—how long has she been standing there in the door? How much did she hear? And also, what are the chances she'd let us put a bell on her expensive-looking shoes so we can hear her coming from now on?

"Ray-Ray, are you ready for our first chess game?" she says.

"You know it," Ray-Ray says. "Don't worry, Dr. Y. I got this."

He's acting just as cool and confident as he tells me to be all the time. So maybe Ray-Ray's a decent teacher after all.

Because even I believe him.

RAY-RAY VS. DR. Y.

I shouldn't have believed him. Ray-Ray and Dr. Yetty's game lasts about forty-five seconds. That bamma didn't stand a chance.

He puts a pawn out. She puts a pawn out.

Ray-Ray moves his knight. She moves her bishop.

Then Ray-Ray stops and looks around. His knee is bouncing up and down, and I can tell he's trying to figure something out.

The rules are, he has to get through a game—win, lose, or draw, but without asking any questions or making any illegal moves.

And I can't say a word. Dr. Yetty told me I could watch, but I have to sit behind Ray-Ray and keep my mouth shut. I'm keeping my fingers crossed, too. This is my chance to put all this Ray-Ray stuff behind me, once and for all.

Then on his third move, Ray-Ray jumps his queen over some pawns and sets her down on the other side. In chess, that's about as legal as setting the board on fire. And I'm like, *Dude...really?*

"Are you sure about that?" Dr. Yetty asks him before he takes his hand off the queen.

And now I'm like, *Dude...what the...*

Ray-Ray looks at her. He smiles like she's trying to psych him out. Then he takes his hand off the queen and sits back.

"I'm sorry, Ray-Ray," Dr. Yetty tells him. "That's not right."

"Aw, man, I thought I had it," Ray-Ray says.

I thought he had it, too. But that wrong move came out of nowhere.

"Let's give it another week and try again," Dr. Yetty tells us. "Kenny won't let you down. Besides, I believe in second, third, and fourth chances, as long as you're working to get better."

Some other grown-up might have cut us some slack during the match, but not her. She's already standing up to leave. She turns to walk out and all we hear is the *click-clack* of her heels, and then nothing. She's gone.

With Dr. Yetty, the rules are the rules. A deal's a deal.

And that's that.

44

RAY-RAY'S CRIB

Since I'm grounded, I've got to get straight home. Ray-Ray walks with me up Good Hope Road, like he's got nowhere else to be. I'm thinking, *Maybe he has homework to do.* Then I start thinking, *Maybe this fool has something else brewing in that whacked-out, crazy brain of his.*

"Yo, over here," he says all of a sudden.

He crosses the street and goes up to this door between two stores. There used to be an intercom and a lock, but they're broken now. Inside, there's some dusty old stairs and I don't know what else.

"Come on up," he says.

"Do you live here?" I say.

"Nah, man, this is the bank where I work," he says. "Yeah, I live here. Why?"

The truth is, I'm thinking I'm glad *I* don't live here. The stairs kind of creep me out.

"No reason," I say. I don't want him to think I'm dissing him or anything, so I follow him up. In fact, I stick close.

Upstairs, there's a door with a lock, and Ray-Ray uses a key to let us inside.

"Yo, Nicky, you here?" he calls out, but nobody answers. "Guess he's not home," he says, and throws his backpack onto a mattress sitting on the floor. I guess that's where Ray-Ray sleeps.

"Who else lives here?" I say.

"It's just me and Nicky," Ray-Ray tells me. "He's twenty-two, so he can sign my permission slips and stuff. It's no big thing."

"You got a mom or a dad?" I ask him.

"Everyone's got a mom or a dad," Ray-Ray says. Which isn't the same thing as a yes.

Besides the mattress on the floor, there isn't much. The only artwork on the walls are posters of WWE wrestlers, UFC fighters, and NFL quarterbacks like Cam Newton, Colin Kaepernick, Russell Wilson, and of course ya boy RGIII. By the window there's a few pics of Rihanna and Beyoncé Scotch-taped on the wall. There's a bathroom, another door with a padlock on it, and a kitchen right there, but the fridge isn't even plugged in.

I think I'm starting to get the picture here. Like for instance, why Ray-Ray's always bumming for food. Or why he might want to stick around after school, even if it means getting detention, or learning chess.

Or...*not* learning chess, I guess.

"Listen, I've got to go," I say.

"Just hang out," he tells me.

"I can't. G-ma's been on me like white on rice. But you can swing through. You know...if you want dinner," I say. I don't smell anything cooking like I do at our house when I come home from school, and there's nothing in the fridge.

Well, you *know* I don't have to ask Ray-Ray
twice about that. He follows me right back outside
and up the street. He doesn't even say anything
until we're almost home.

Then he says, "You sure your gramma won't mind?"

I look over at Ray-Ray. He's got this big shirt on,
and it makes him look like a pole with a big walnut
head holding up a tent. I don't think I ever noticed
how skinny he is until now.

"G-ma won't mind," I say, "You're good."

45

BOOKS ARE FOR EVERYONE

G-ma doesn't even blink about Ray-Ray. You ask her for some grub, and she'll hook you up.

Once we're inside, Ray-Ray stops and stares at the jillion books we have, on every shelf, on every table, some on the floor, on the couch. Everywhere. Everywhere except for the kitchen table. The only book allowed on the kitchen table is the Bible. That's it.

"What do you like to read, Raymond?" G-ma says from the kitchen. She's in there stirring a pot of her amazing black-eyed peas on the stove. She is the queen of what we call "new" soul food. No butter, no fatback, and instead of flavoring her peas with greasy ham hocks, she uses smoked

turkey. (But to keep it real, I still call it a Two-Toot Special because of all the beans.)

"I dunno," Ray-Ray says.

"What do you mean, you don't know?" G-ma asks. "Everyone has something they like to read."

He just shrugs. "I don't mean to be rude or nothing, but...books are for sissies," he says. "The only people I know who read are girls."

"Uh-oh" is all I say. Too bad Ray-Ray didn't bring a crash helmet. I think he's about to need one.

But G-ma keeps her cool. Ray-Ray's a guest, after all.

"You listen to me, Raymond," she says. "I don't know what makes you think that way, but books are for *everyone*, including you." She pulls one off the shelf. It's *Roll of Thunder, Hear My Cry*. "You take this," she says.

"No thanks," he says, but G-ma gives him another one of her looks. It says, *Oh, no, you didn't*, and *We're not done here*, and *I may be small, but I can get nuclear mad if I have to*, all at the same time. I guess Ray-Ray picks up on it, because he keeps hold of that book.

"Now come over here," she says, and gives him another one out of the living room.

"And…here," she says, going straight into my room.

Five minutes later, Ray-Ray's all loaded down with *Hatchet*, *Harry Potter*, and *The Giver*, too.

"Next week, you come back here for dinner, and I want to hear about at least one of those books," she says. "If you can't find something to like in that stack, I say you're not trying hard enough. You hear me?"

Ray-Ray shrugs. "Yeah," he says.

"Excuse me? 'Yeah' is not a word," G-ma says.

"Yes, ma'am," Ray-Ray says.

So I guess he's starting to see where the whole *Grandma's Boy* thing came from. To be honest, I kind of like it. It's like I'm getting the night off.

And the weird part is, I think Ray-Ray likes it, too. I guess everyone can use a little G-ma now and then.

Plus, that Two-Toot Special is really good.

THE WHOLE TRUTH AND NOTHING BUT THE TRUTH (ABOUT MY DAD)

While G-ma's getting dinner ready, I take Ray-Ray in my room and show him my comic collection. I know he thinks I'm a geek for reading them, but I give him a couple of the New 52 to take home with the other books. I'm a huge DC Comics fan. Marvel is cool, but I've been a DC head, Justice League and all that stuff, since I was a little kid.

"Just try them," I say, but then I shut up because now I'm starting to sound like G-ma.

"Who's this?" Ray-Ray asks me next. He picks up the picture of my dad from next to the bed.

It's an old picture, and it shows him in his good

police uniform. "Dress blues" is what Dad used to call them.

"That's my father," I say.

"I thought you said he was some kind of big detective," Ray-Ray says.

Oh, man. I've got so many lies going, I kind of forgot about this one. So I take a risk—a huge risk—and go ahead and tell Ray-Ray the truth.

"He was," I say. "But then he died. Some guy shot him in the stomach when he was making an arrest. Like three years ago."

"For real?" Ray-Ray says.

"His name was Kenneth Wright, like me," I say. "He's the one who taught me how to play chess."

Ray-Ray doesn't say anything about that. He doesn't call me out about lying, either. Which is cool.

It's not like I meant to keep it all a secret. Arthur knows about it. Dele and Vashon, too. I just don't like to talk about it that much. G-ma always says I'm the bravest kid she knows, because of everything that happened. But back then, it didn't make me feel so brave. Kind of the opposite, actually.

"Dude looks like you," Ray-Ray says. Then he

sets the picture down again and picks up one of my comics.

"I guess," I say. People used to tell me that all the time.

Mostly, though, I think he looks like Stainlezz Steel.

PUBLIC ENEMY #1

CRAY-CRAY COMES THROUGH

ANOTHER ONE BITES THE DUST

*T*he next morning when G-ma walks me to
school, Dr. Yetty isn't standing outside.
Usually, she's right there, saying good morning
and asking everyone if they did their homework.

But not today.

Then during homeroom, Mrs. Freeman gets
on the loudspeakers and does the morning
announcements instead of Dr. Yetty. I'm thinking
she must be sick at home—like really sick. Dr. Y. is
the type of principal who would come to school in a
tornado if she could.

But it turns out to be something even worse.

During second-period math, the door opens and
Mrs. Freeman comes in with some old dude I've

never seen before. He's wearing a suit, a tie, and a smile that has *bad news* written all over it.

"Good morning, boys and girls," Mrs. Freeman says. "I'd like to introduce you to Mr. Bowman, our new principal here at UMS...."

There's some more yakkety-yak after that, but I don't hear it. I'm just thinking, *New principal? Seriously?*

This is the third principal of the year and it's not even Christmas yet! Mr. Diaw lasted about five

minutes. Dr. Yetty lasted about ten. It's like they've got a revolving door on that office.

PRINCIPAL
~~SMITH~~
~~MONTGOMERY~~
~~JACKSON~~
~~BLOOM~~
~~DIAW~~
~~YETTY~~
BOWMAN

Meanwhile, everyone's talking at once. Tiny and Jerome are high-fiving. Ms. Jones looks like she wants to cry. And Lucinda Morehead *is* crying. She really liked Dr. Yetty. So did I.

Mrs. Freeman claps her hands to get us all quiet, but I speak up anyway. "Where's Dr. Yetty?" I say.

That's when the new guy steps up. He still has that smile stuck on his face, like someone painted it there.

"Due to an emergency situation at Southridge Elementary, Dr. Yetty has been transferred over to that school," he says, and then some other stuff I don't listen to. I'm back inside my head, trying to figure out what this all means.

I'm almost eighty-seven percent certain that Dr. Yetty being transferred has something to do with the handful of (and I'm sorry for saying this) stupid-thinking parents who complained about the good things she brought to the school. I bet you!

Mr. Bowman fixes his goofy-looking mouth to say something else I'll just ignore. But before he can spit out one syllable, he's interrupted by what sounds like a sea of anger flooding the hallways.

We all get up and rush to the door to see over a hundred hollering, fussing, cussing, and just plain old upset parents, grandparents, aunts, and uncles. It looks like the whole neighborhood is there. It's a sight to see, and hear. And man, does it bring a smile to my face.

"WE WANT DR. YETTY BACK!"

"WHAT SENSE DOES THIS MAKE TO PULL THE LADY OUT SO SOON!?"

"WE'RE NOT GOING TO STAND FOR THIS ANYMORE! THE SCHOOL DISTRICT THINKS THEY CAN DO US ANY KIND OF WAY. NOT THIS TIME!"

I'm filled with pride, mixed with more anger. I feel like a dude who's in a fight and his hands are tied up. *Somebody has to do something*, is my first thought.

Basically, there's two things I know for sure.

One—G-ma's going to be *ticked*. And I mean like super-nuclear mad with extra crazy mambo sauce. As far as she's concerned, Dr. Yetty's the only good thing to happen at UMS in a long time.

And two—no more chess lessons for me and Ray-Ray! If Dr. Yetty's gone, then the deal is off. And to be real, I don't know how I feel about that.

Because the rest of it feels like a first-round uppercut knockout punch from Floyd Mayweather for poor old Union Middle School. But seeing all of them in the hallway, standing up for us, kind of loosens the ties around my hands. Union might be down for a second, but I feel like I'm going to help it get back to its feet and come out of our corner swinging.

Haymakers, baby.

SPLAT!

All day long, I can't find Ray-Ray around school. Then at 3:15, I'm headed out and I see him coming up the sidewalk toward the front entrance.

"Yo, where you going?" he says.

"Home," I say. "Where have you been all day?"

"Around. Mind your own, son," he tells me.

I guess Ray-Ray doesn't worry about skipping school. His brother probably writes him all the excuse notes he wants.

> Ray-Ray wasn't
> in school
> today.
> You got A
> problem with
> that? Yeah,
> didn't
> think so.
> NICKY P.

So I tell Ray-Ray about Dr. Yetty and the huge crowd that came up to represent for her. I also mention how we might be off the hook for those chess lessons. But when I try to give him some dap, Ray-Ray just leaves me hanging.

"What's wrong?" I ask him.

"Nothing," Ray-Ray says, but you can tell it's more like the opposite. I guess he's too cool to let me know how he really feels. It's not like I'm Dr. Phil or something.

"Ray-Ray? You good?" I say.

"I'll see you later," he says. "I gotta bounce."

"No you don't," I tell him. "You were just coming here to meet me. What's the deal?"

Ray-Ray stops again and turns around. He ice-grills me like he wants to give me one of John Cena's Attitude Adjustments. I'm talking a *painful*-looking frown.

"Put it this way," he says. "You're way better at teaching chess than you thought."

"Huh?" I say.

"You think I jacked up that game with Dr. Yetty by accident?" he asks me.

"Uh...kind of," I say.

Now my head's spinning. If Ray-Ray blew that game on purpose, that means he wants those chess lessons to keep going. And maybe not just because of the snacks.

"You want to play some now?" I ask him. "I can go get my set."

"Nah, man," he says, and backs off. "I'm good. You just do you. I just thought we were cool."

"We are," I say.

"Yeah, as long as it gets you out of trouble. After that, you just leave me hangin', right? I see how you do it."

It's like I've got this new superpower, and it's all about making people mad at me. I don't even have to try anymore.

"Ray-Ray, hold up," I say. "That ain't it."

But he's already running. There's a bus on the curb just up the street. Ray-Ray jumps on the back, grabs hold, and hitches a ride.

"Stop buggin' out!" I yell at him. "You're acting like a real punk right now!" Which is probably the wrong thing to say.

That's when Ray-Ray looks over at me and ice-grills me again. The problem is, that bus is about to take a corner, and Ray-Ray's too busy squinting his eyes, trying to shoot hot laser beams at me like Cyclops or something. I wish he'd kept his eyes on the bus.

He takes one hand off the back and does something real rude with it just as the bus swings around that corner. Ray-Ray loses his grip.

When he falls, it's like slow motion. All I can do is watch while he goes down—and hits the street. Hard. His head bangs into the concrete, and it sounds like someone hitting a pumpkin with a hammer. I don't think I'll ever forget that sound.

After that, Ray-Ray's out. Like a light.

51

I HATE HOSPITALS!

I used Ray-Ray's phone to call 911. Then
G-ma. Then Nicky, but he didn't pick up,
so I left a message.

Now I'm at the hospital with G-ma, and we're
waiting to find out if Ray-Ray has to spend the
night, or needs a new skull, or will spend the rest
of his life sucking burgers through a straw. So far,
there's no sign of Nicky at all.

G-ma's talking to the people at the desk while
I'm sitting here waiting...and waiting...and
waiting. No wonder they call it the waiting room,
'cause that's all that happens here. I didn't bring a
book, plus I only have one game for my PS Vita—
but I can't concentrate on anything anyway.

I hate this place. There's sick people everywhere.
Some of them have broken bones. Some of them

are lying on stretchers. And maybe you don't see it, but you just know there's dead people around here somewhere, peeping around corners and stuff. I mean, seriously, does anyone *like* hospitals?

The other thing is, this is the hospital where my dad died. It was a long time ago, and I wasn't here when it happened. But that doesn't stop G-ma from treating me like a baby. She keeps asking if I want to go to my aunt Nina's while she gets this figured out.

The thing is, I *want* to be here. It's not like what happened to Ray-Ray is my fault—but it's not exactly *not* my fault, either. If I'm lucky, banging that big wrecking ball of his on the concrete gave him amnesia. Maybe he'll forget he was ever mad at me in the first place.

Finally, G-ma brings over some visitor passes and I follow her down the hall. They've got Ray-Ray in one of those little rooms with curtains for walls, and his head is wrapped up with about a mile of white bandages. He looks like a human Q-tip, but I don't say so.

Ray-Ray stares at me for a second, like he can't decide if he's still mad, or what.

"We cool?" I ask him.

He just shrugs, but I think he means yes. "Did anyone call my brother?" he asks.

"I'm sure he'll be here soon, dear," G-ma says, and touches his cheek like she does with mine sometimes. "How are you feeling?"

He drops the obvious. "My head hurts."

That cracks me up. I can't help it, but it's okay, because then Ray-Ray starts laughing, too. The only one who doesn't even smile is G-ma.

"Buses aren't toys, Raymond," she says. "You have to make better decisions from now on, baby. Next time you might not be so lucky. Walk away with the good sense God gave you. You hear me?"

"Yes, ma'am," Ray-Ray says, even though he's still cheesing over at me.

"What were you two doing outside, anyway?" G-ma asks. "Why weren't you having chess club today?"

And I'm like, *Oh, great.* I got things smoothed over with Ray-Ray about half a second ago, and I'm already running into another lie.

"It's not chess club," I tell her. "It's just chess."

"That's not what I asked," G-ma says.

She's got her back to Ray-Ray, and he's watching me like TV. He's not snitching me out about the deal with Dr. Yetty, but he's not helping out, either. So maybe he's still a *little* mad.

Then before I can mess things up any more, I get a lucky break. That curtain pulls back, and Nicky Powell is standing there.

"What's up, baby bruh?" Nicky says. "You good?"

Ray-Ray sits up a little straighter. "I'm cool," he says. "I'll bounce right back. You know me, Nick."

"No doubt," Nicky says, and starts to give him a pound and a hug.

"Ouch!" Ray-Ray says.

Meanwhile, G-ma's staring at Nicky like she's thinking, *Where the heck have you been?* But she keeps it polite.

"You must be Raymond's brother," she says. "I'm Hope Wright. And this is my grandson—"

"Chess Man!" Nicky says, and shakes my hand while G-ma looks surprised that Nicky shows me some love.

"Do you two know each other?" G-ma says.

Well, you know that expression—out of the frying pan and into the fire? That's me. Pants on fire. Engulfed in flames. Total cremation.

Before Nicky can jump in, I answer real quick. "Nicky picks Ray-Ray up at school sometimes," I say. "That's all."

I can't even look at Ray-Ray right now. If G-ma finds out I went riding with Nicky and Trayvon that day, *I'm* going to be the next one checking into the hospital.

Seriously, I don't know how much more of this I can take. So I make a promise to myself, right there. *No more lying to G-ma.* Well…no more *new* lies, anyway. I can't undo all the old ones yet. Not without starting World War III.

But no new ones. I'm putting that on everything. I'm going to change. That's my word.

I just hope I'm telling myself the truth right now.

I always want to do right, but you know…for whatever reason…it doesn't turn out that way.

FULL STEAM AHEAD

When we leave the hospital, we don't even go home. We head straight over to St. Anthony's Church for an emergency neighborhood meeting.

Word's gotten around about Dr. Yetty, and I guess that was the last straw. This whole action thing with the big march and the rally is going on ahead of schedule—like *tomorrow*.

And that means I've got less than twenty-four hours to figure out what I'm going to say in front of all those people.

"Look who it is—our student ambassador!" Mrs. Clark says when we come in. A bunch of people start clapping again, and I'm thinking they should save all that for someone who deserves it.

"I know it's last-minute," G-ma tells me, "so you don't have to speak at the rally if you don't want to."

"Yes he does!" voices that I recognize yell out. It's Vashon and Dele.

"Kenny really has a lot to say. He's smart. I know he'll say what we all want to hear," Vashon vouches for me.

Dele turns to me and says, "You'll be our voice, bro. The students."

That just blows me away. They both give me a pound and a pat on the back. It's kind of weird, but really cool at the same time. You know? They're looking at me like I could be some sort of savior. I wouldn't go that far, but hearing them have my back really puts a little more pressure on the situation.

But here's the weird thing. It makes me *want* to do the speech even more. I mean, don't get me wrong. I'm still as scared as a dude standing at the doorstep of a cute girl's house when her gigantic father answers the door gritting his teeth and growling like a pit bull.

But I feel like I owe G-ma big-time, after all the lying and everything. This is my chance to get it right. I feel like the kids at UMS are depending on me. And even though she didn't say so, Dr. Yetty needs me to say something important. I have to get to work.

The good news is, they got a bunch of pizza for the meeting, and I'm starving. G-ma tells me to grab some food and go find a quiet spot to "gather my thoughts."

So that's what I do. I wind up in the churchy part of the church. You know, where the Mother's Board sits, right across from the pulpit and the choir stand.

I don't know if you're supposed to eat pizza in here, but hopefully God won't mind. It's hard to pray on an empty stomach, and I figure a prayer or two couldn't hurt right about now. Because I need some answers.

Like about what I'm going to say tomorrow.

And how I'm going to stop lying to G-ma for real.

And make Arthur my best friend again.

And make sure Ray-Ray's okay, too.

I can't help it. All these thoughts are running through my head all at once. It's like a traffic jam in my brain.

And that's when I hear this voice out of nowhere—

No kidding, I'm like, *God?* I'm also thinking
God's a lady, because she sounds a whole lot like
Dr. Yetty. (But you're already way ahead of me on
this, aren't you?)

I turn around and there she is, standing
behind me with a paper plate and a piece of pizza.
Seriously, nobody can sneak into
a room like Dr. Yetty James.

"I just saw your grandma,"
she says. "Sounds like you
had a rough day."

"Not as rough as Ray-Ray," I say, and she comes over to sit down.

"Are you ever coming back to UMS?" I ask her, straight up.

She gives me a straight-up answer. "I'm sorry, Kenny, but it's not my choice."

"Are you coming to the big thing tomorrow?" I ask.

But she just shakes her head. "I don't think it would be appropriate. That's why I'm here tonight. I want to help however I can."

"Well, I want to give a good speech," I say. "And most of all...I want to help bring you back to UMS. Your school."

Her eyes get a little misty. Just a little, as she smiles at me like she's looking at Steel. And it's the first time I've ever seen her speechless. I think she knows I mean what I say.

"What have you got so far?" she asks me.

I look down at my notebook. All I have on the page are a couple of pepperoni-scented grease stains.

"Not too sure how I should set it off," I say. "I don't even know how I'm supposed to put all these thoughts in my head on paper."

I DON'T KNOW WHAT HE'S GOING TO SAY, BUT IT SMELLS DELICIOUS.

MY BIG SPEECH!

I feel like turning my head sideways, tapping it, and watching every single word fall gently on my notebook—in my best handwriting ever. But that ain't gonna happen.

"Maybe that's the wrong question," Dr. Yetty says. "Forget about *supposed to*. What do you *want to* say, Kenny?"

I think about that for a second.

And then she says something that sparks me.

"Do you remember, in the second week of my history class, when we discussed Dr. King's address to the Montgomery Improvement Association? 1955?"

See, everyone always mentions the "I Have a Dream" speech, which was a big deal. But they never give any love to the speech that started it all. "You know it," I told her. "It was his first major speech. Like this one is for me."

"Yes, and rumor has it that he only had twenty minutes to prepare it. He spoke from the heart. He spoke for those people just fighting for human rights. He spoke for the people."

"G-ma says I should tell my own story," I say. "And my story is—I guess, a part of everyone else's story who lives here."

Dr. Yetty smiles. "You can't go wrong there," she says. "If you speak from the heart, it's always true." She hands me a napkin to wipe the trail of grease from my chin and adds, "What Dr. King was most concerned about in that speech was what he could say to keep the people courageous and prepared for a positive outcome. You have to speak a positive outcome into existence, Kenny."

"But that doesn't mean it's going to be easy," I say. "To keep it real—I'm pretty scared about the whole thing. You know?"

She takes a bite of pizza and doesn't answer at first. Then she says, "There's an expression I love. It says, 'Speak the truth, even if your voice shakes.' So let it shake, Kenny. That's okay. Sometimes courage feels a whole lot like being scared."

I like that. Dr. Yetty doesn't try to pretend things are different than they are. She doesn't sugarcoat stuff, either, that's for sure.

But I'm also starting to figure out exactly what I want to say tomorrow.

Hopefully. Positive, positive outcomes.

53

MARCH ISN'T JUST A MONTH OF THE YEAR

*T*he next day after school is crazy! They have signs pointing the way when we get out for the day, and parents are herding kids over to the start of the march. There are police along the road and news cameras getting ready to film the whole thing.

I see Arthur in the crowd and tap him on the shoulder.

"You want to walk over there together?" I say.

And he's like, "I'll just see you there," which is what I said to him on the way to that field trip. I guess I deserve that.

When we get to the corner of MLK Ave (which is kinda poetic, seeing how I just had that conversation about speeches and stuff with

Dr. Yetty) and Good Hope Road, it's all blocked off and there's people *everywhere*. Not just from my school, but all over. I don't recognize half of them. This thing's gonna be huge.

G-ma actually gets the whole thing going. When everyone's lined up and holding on to their signs, and ready to march, she stands up on the bumper of a car with this big old bullhorn, while Vashon's dad and I hold her steady. She's so small up there, she looks like a little hood ornament—but a mighty hood ornament. She looks like Sojourner Truth or Shirley Chisholm. But it's my grandmother.

My grandmother.

Once she gets that bullhorn going, she sounds huge.

"WHAT DO WE WANT?" G-ma says.

"Great schools!" a bunch of people say back.

"WHAT DO WE WANT?" G-ma says again.

"GREAT SCHOOLS!" a whole lot more people say, all at the same time.

"AND WHEN DO WE WANT IT?"

"Now!" everyone says.

"WHEN DO WE WANT IT?" G-ma yells.

"NOW!" they say.

The crowd is fired up. I'm shouting, too. It feels good to let off some steam, even if it all seems kind of unrealistic. I mean, I don't know how GREAT Union Middle School is ever going to get—and I definitely don't think it's going to happen NOW.

But I'll tell you what else. Once all those people—all of *us*—start marching up MLK Ave, it feels like we can do *anything*.

WHAT DO WE WANT?

MY SPEECH (MORE ABOUT THAT LATER)

HERE GOES NOTHING

By the time we get to the school, people are fired UP! They've got a podium on the steps, and a microphone with a real sound system, and everything.

The mayor gets his picture taken with a bunch of kids, but I'm too nervous for that. Plus, I don't know if I'd want to do that anyway. I'm sure he's a cool dude, but would he come by and take a picture with us, have lunch, and shake our hands if we weren't marching? I'm just saying.

They want me to talk first, and maybe that's a good thing. I just need to get this over with.

Pretty soon, Mrs. Clark gets up and introduces me and tells everyone that I'd like to say a few words.

Really? I'm not so sure about that. More like I'd

like to *not* have a kindergarten flashback to when I peed all down my leg during a Christmas play. (I made a big enough puddle for Lawona Bigelow to slip and fall into the front row.) I'm *that* kind of scared. But it's too late to back out.

Next thing I know, I'm walking up to that podium and facing off with the biggest crowd of people you've ever seen.

"Um…hi," I say into the mike, and my voice booms out, all the way to Virginia. My heart's ready to explode, and my throat's as dry as some of Ray-Ray's jokes. Also, my mind's a total blank. I can't remember what I want to say!

But then I remember that greasy piece of notebook paper in my back pocket, and I pull it out. My whole speech is right there. I think about how Dr. King must have felt when he addressed that crowd in 1955.

I take a deep breath. Swallow hard. And start to talk.

"I just want to say…Dr. Yetty is the best principal I've ever had," I tell everyone. "Don't we deserve to have a good principal? Don't we!? Just one? Not a new one every year. It's called consistency, or something like that, right?"

The crowd roars, "YEAH!" and "YOU TELL 'EM, LITTLE BROTHA!" Some people even cheer and applaud, too. And G-ma's smiling at me from the front row like I'm the next Stokely Carmichael or something (look him up).

But I'm just getting started. It's time for me to do what I came here to do.

Time to tell the truth.

"Dr. Yetty took a chance on me," I say. "When she could have given me a suspension, she told me I could teach chess instead."

A couple of people clap at that, but nobody cheers.

G-ma's not exactly smiling anymore, either. I can't even look at her now. So I look around for Arthur, Dele, and Vashon instead, and I keep on talking.

"I'm not perfect and I haven't been a perfect friend or grandson, but I'm getting better at that. I'm working on all of that. Really. I want to be someone they can rely on. I'd also like to tell my grandma the truth a little more often."

I decide to get back on track a little after a few people in the front look at me sideways. "But you know who else could do better?" I ask the crowd.

And they respond with a loud "WHO!?!"

And I say, "The people who run our schools!" That gets another giant cheer.

"You're supposed to stand by your friends and do right by your family. I didn't do that for a little while. Just like the district people. They need to stand by our school, all of the schools. They need to do right by us kids, do right by our families and our whole community!"

More people are applauding now. I see Arthur off to the side, and he isn't clapping, but he's listening, anyway. And even though G-ma's steaming away, right there in the front row, I feel like someone's lifting weights off me, ten pounds at a time. I'm about ready to take off like a balloon.

I'm almost done, too.

"I can't begin to tell you how many principals I've had ever since I've been in school. Not-so-good ones. Bad ones. You name it. But when we finally get one that fits, a perfect fit, they snatch her away. Y'all know that's not right," I say before I yank the mike off the stand and begin to walk around. "Not only is it not right—it *ain't* right!"

The crowd goes nuts after that one. I keep going.

"We should clone people like Dr. Yetty and put her in every school. My grandma, who's standing right there"—I point at her, but she keeps a stone face—"she always says, how can you educate or lead anyone if you don't understand or care about where they're coming from…or where they're going? Dr. Yetty cares about both."

I'm really feeling it now. I don't know where it comes from, but it just kind of falls out of my mouth. "And we *demand* that she be transferred back to Union Middle School—immediately. There is no way the school can be everything it can be without her!"

And since I'm on a roll, I decide to just empty my soul or guts. Whichever one sounds cooler.

"So before I close out, I just want to say I'm sorry to everyone I've done wrong by, especially my grandma, who does everything for me. She takes care of me, makes sure I'm not doing stupid stuff. She drives me to be better. She's like my guardian angel, and she took me in when no one else would. What if she had treated me how Union has been dogged out, or how the rest of the schools here have been treated? I wouldn't be standing in front of you now. I don't know where I'd be...."

I look down at G-ma and then close out. "Things are going to change. That's a promise. How about, instead of those district people making all the decisions about how our schools should be run, why can't people like my grandma, like Dr. Yetty"—and then I point out into the massive crowd—"people like YOU decide? I mean...who knows better about what the schools need than you?"

They all yell in one big voice, "NOBODY!"

"That's right. The decisions should be yours. Power. To. The people. And—um...that's all. Thanks!" I tell the crowd.

I step off the little box where I'm standing, but everyone's still cheering louder than ever. A bunch of people shout my name, too, and the mayor shakes my hand. Why not? I shake it back.

It's a weird feeling. Weird, and amazing. There's a thousand people out there clapping for me, and all I did was give a little speech. The mayor's standing next to me, and the cameras are rolling, and even though I still have G-ma to worry about, I'm not going to lie.

I feel just a little bit like a hero.

TIME TO COME CLEAN

I'm on TV that night. There's a whole story about the march on the news, and they even show me talking for about ten seconds. I'm famous! It's awesome...

…for about ten seconds. Then it's time for G-ma and me to have a big talk.

Actually, I do most of the talking. I tell her about everything—from that first detention, to that car ride with Nicky, to the *real* reason Ray-Ray and I weren't playing chess yesterday. G-ma doesn't like it, but she listens long enough to let me get through it.

"I'm really sorry, G-ma," I tell her. "I lied way too much."

"One lie is too many," she says, and I guess I can't argue with that.

"I'll take whatever punishment you have to give me," I say. "But there's something else I want to say first."

"Haven't you said enough?" she asks me.

Still, I keep going. "You need to figure out that I'm not a little kid anymore. I'm eleven years old—"

"And eight months, and twenty-two days," she says. "What does that have to do with lying, Kenneth?"

"Part of this—a lot of it, actually—has to do with what they call me at school," I tell her. I know she's not going to like this, but I can't turn back now. "Grandma's Boy," I say.

"What's wrong with that?" she says. She even looks kind of hurt. "Why would they think that's something to be ashamed of?"

"See? This is part of the problem," I tell her. "I mean...I like being your grandson. And I *am* Grandma's Boy, here at home. But out there? At school? I need to start growing up. And you need to understand that."

"You're still a child, Kenneth," she says. "Not a grown-up. Not yet."

"But I will be someday," I say. "And I *am* the man of this house."

I stop there because it's making me think about my dad, and how I'll have to grow up the rest of the way without him.

But hey, if I'm lucky—if I'm really, really lucky— then I'll be a whole lot like him when I get there. As much as I can, anyway. I don't know if anyone can fill those shoes. But the thing I'm trying to tell G-ma is that I want to try.

I think she gets it, because she's crying, too. Not a lot. G-ma almost never cries. Still, I can see she's holding back some tears, trying to be strong for me like she always does.

"Even though you're the only *male* in the house, that doesn't make you the *man* of the house," G-ma says.

"Aren't they the same thing?" I ask. I mean, really, aren't they?

"You're going to grow up to be a fine man someday, Kenneth. But take your time. Enjoy being eleven. Enjoy the ins and outs, the ups and downs, and the bumps and bruises you'll receive becoming a man," G-ma says in a clear but trembling voice.

"And…there's one more thing," I say. "I want to walk to school by myself from now on. Is that okay?"

G-ma puts an arm around me and pulls me in close. She takes a deep breath and says, "All right. I'll think about that."

Which is pretty close to a yes, if you know G-ma.

"Cool," I say.

"Just as soon as you're un-grounded," she says. "Maybe after Christmas."

And I'm like, *What?* "But I told the truth!" I tell her. "The whole truth!"

"Telling the truth isn't an extra-credit assignment," G-ma says. "It's what grown-ups are supposed to do."

"But—" I say, before she keeps going.

"Your steps are made of stone, Kenneth," G-ma says. She turns sideways on the couch now and looks me right in the eye. "Always remember that. Whichever ones you choose to take—that's it. The truth of those steps stays behind you, hard as rock. Forever. You have to live with them, consequences and all."

I don't say anything to that. I know G-ma's

making sense, and I know I'm going to have to be grounded, like it or not. Once she decides something, that's pretty much it.

But there is one thing she got wrong. My steps aren't made of stone.

They're made of steel.

56

FACE-OFF

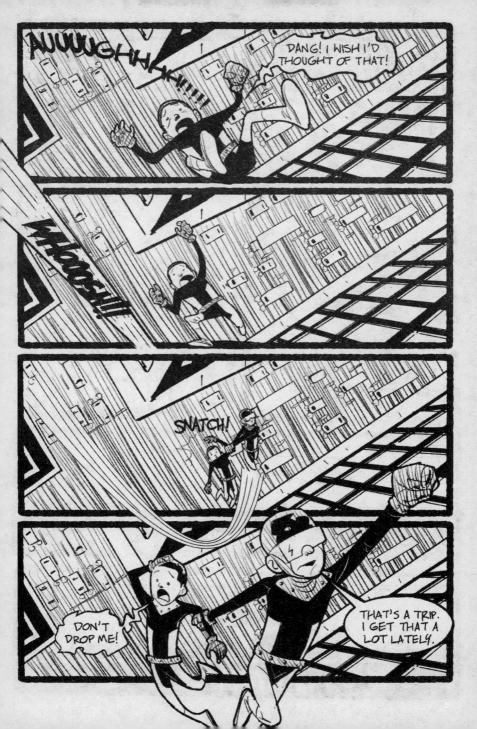

57

YOU NEVER KNOW

P*op quiz!*

Question: What has two thumbs and just got invited by the mayor of Washington, DC, to be part of his new Student Advisory Council?

Answer:

THAT'S RIGHT—YA BOY K-DUB!

I guess the mayor liked what I said in that speech. A few days after the big rally, I got an official letter in the mail. It said they were starting this thing up and wanted me to be part of it. We're like "boys" now, the mayor and me.

Now a bunch of kids from all over the city and I are supposed to meet once a month and come up with ideas to tell the district about how they can make school better for everyone. Crazy, right?

I don't know what I'm going to say yet, but G-ma tells me to think big. So that's what I'm doing. Maybe we could get a new gym at UMS. Or at least enough desks for everyone to sit down in class. And some books that aren't a hundred years old once in a while. Let's try harder to keep the awesome teachers and principals we already have, like Dr. Yetty, and replace the handful of poseurs who don't have a clue.

Speaking of which, guess who's back at UMS? That's right—Dr. Yetty, baby!

We did it! And I'd like to think my speech had a little something to do with it. Just a little.

And who knows? Maybe…just maybe…this is the start of something even bigger for me. Maybe

I'll play a part in making things better in the whole city. You never know.

I'm not saying this is going to turn me into some kind of big shot overnight. But then again, I never thought I'd give a speech to a thousand people, or get a letter from City Hall addressed to *me*. So who knows? Maybe G-ma's right. Maybe thinking big isn't such a bad idea.

Meanwhile, things at school are going okay. Ray-Ray had his head shaved when he got out of the hospital, but he's the same otherwise. He still talks all the time, and he never stops fidgeting. It just doesn't bug me like it used to.

And Arthur and I are cool again, too. We're back to playing chess whenever we can. I save lunch and after-school for him. Ray-Ray and I play at other times. He comes over for dinner a couple of days a week now, so we usually get in a few games then. Even Nicky and Trayvon have dropped by to get their grub on. Crazy, right? I know.

Which brings me up to the next problem.

It's Tuesday at 6:30, and Ray-Ray's nowhere in sight. G-ma's making spaghetti and meatballs tonight. There's no way Ray-Ray's passing that up on purpose.

When I saw him at school today, everything was okay, so I don't know what's going on now. He's not picking up his phone, either. And even though I'm still grounded, G-ma says I can run over there to see if Ray-Ray's home.

So that's what I'm going to do. But I don't have a good feeling about this.

ANYBODY HOME?

I know the door from the street is going to be unlocked when I get to Ray-Ray's. And those stairs still creep me out.

But when I get up to his apartment door, that's open, too. Which is weird. Usually, Ray-Ray and Nicky keep that one locked.

That's when I see the knob is broken off. The door frame is busted up, too. I'm thinking maybe I should just turn around and go tell G-ma.

Until I hear someone crying inside.

Now I feel really weird, but I can't just leave. So I push that door open a little more and look in.

"Hello?" I say.

Ray-Ray sits up quick. He's on his mattress on the floor, and obviously he was the one crying. But he tries to act cool now.

"Wassup?" he says.

"That's what I was going to ask you," I say. When I look over, that padlock on Nicky's door is busted, too. And there's no sign of Nicky, either.

"Ray-Ray, what happened here, dude?" I say.

Ray-Ray takes a deep breath. I've seen him mad before, and happy, and hyper, and confused. I just don't think I've ever seen him sad.

"Nicky got locked up," he says. Just like that. "He was gone when I came home, and his room's all messed up. But there's a message on my phone. Police came and took him away."

"What'd he do?" I say.

Ray-Ray shrugs. "He never told me what he was up to. Maybe on purpose."

I don't have a good reason to be scared, but I kind of am now. I'm not sure what to say, or even what to think.

Finally, I ask Ray-Ray, "What happens next?"

"I dunno," he says. "They're probably going to put me in a home or something. I'm kind of out here by myself."

"Nah, man. You've got me," I say, and I sit down next to him. "And you've got G-ma, too."

Ray-Ray just looks at the floor. He doesn't have anything left to say. And while I'm sitting there, I start thinking about G-ma and her starfish story.

The truth is, I don't know when things are going to get better at Union Middle School. Maybe it will be soon, and maybe not. But in the meantime, there's one thing I know I can do for sure. And I don't have to wait another second to get it done.

So I stand up and put out my hand. "Come on," I say to Ray-Ray. "Get your stuff. Right now."

"Where are we going?" he asks me when he gets up.

"Where do you think?" I say. "We're late for dinner."

HOME FOR THE HOLIDAYS

Happy Thanksgiving! Come on in and grab a seat—if you can find one. Our apartment is about as crowded as the National Mall on the Fourth of July. Mad packed from wall to wall. Maybe it just feels that way because we've never had this many people over. It's all good, though.

Mrs. Clark and her family are here. My aunt Nina, too, and my other aunt Sarah and my uncle Carl, and their three little kids. Also, Dr. Yetty and her husband. Who knew she was married? Lucky, lucky man. Who knows, maybe I'll marry a lady as smart and pretty someday.

Preemie and her mom are right over there. They live in a shelter, so G-ma said they should come along. I invited Arthur, too, because his dad has to work at the restaurant today.

And Ray-Ray's here, of course. Where else is he going to be? See, he lives with us now. G-ma's still working out some of the details, but the social worker said we could keep it this way for the time being. He's officially unofficially a part of the family now.

One day, just out of the blue, we received a collect phone call from the DC Department of Corrections. It was Nicky. I don't know how he found our phone number, but hey, it *is* Nicky Powell. The brotha is pretty resourceful.

"It's Nicky, Ray-Ray!" I shouted, and he hopped over the couch in the living room and snatched the phone. They spoke for a good fifteen minutes. Ray-Ray told me Nicky may be out within a year or so. They talk once a week. I don't know how things will change once Nicky gets out. We'll handle that when the time comes.

For now, Ray-Ray has to live by G-ma's rules, same as me. Which is almost funny. He's reading every day, like it or not—mostly not. But he's also seriously getting into my comic collection.

I even told him about Stainlezz Steel. Maybe I shouldn't have, but I did. And get this—he says if I can be Stainlezz Steel in my mind, then he can be someone, too. He says his superhero is called—get this—A Brotha Named Zeus.

I ask him, "Do you mean just Zeus?"

He says, "No, bamma. You gotta say the whole thing. A Brotha Named Zeus. There could be all kinda Zeuses out there in the universe, you understand? But I am"—he points at me and we say it together—"A *Brotha* Named Zeus!" He says that's the name he picked, and he's sticking with it. Who am I to argue? He could call himself Tito Jackson for all I care.

Besides, I have *"young man* of the house" business to tend to. It's just about time to carve the turkey, and you know how much Ray-Ray eats. If I don't get to that table on time, I'll be lucky to get anything at all. He'll smash all the collard greens, G-ma's famous homemade dressing, her amazing sweet potato pie, and my favorite, the fruit salad.

CHESS, ANYONE?

One more surprise. Guess what we have at Union Middle School now?

Chess club! We're doin' it big at Union now, baby. Yeah, seriously. It was my, Arthur's, and Ray-Ray's idea. Anyone who stays after school for detention or whatever, and wants to, can come down the hall and learn chess for an hour. G-ma even paid for some extra chess sets, so we're all good to go.

Of course, that means I'm hanging with the D-Squad a lot more than I was before. And those are the ones I spent the whole beginning of sixth grade trying to stay away from!

But here's the thing. Tiny, and Kwame, and Jerome, and all of them still think I have some secret rep. Like I'm connected to the streets somehow. The way they look at me, they're not even sure I didn't have something to do with sending Nicky Powell to jail. And let's just say that whatever those guys don't know won't hurt them.

No, wait. More like whatever they don't know won't hurt *me*.

So am I going to let them know that I'm just a mild-mannered, easy-to-get-along-with chess geek who's still almost as scared of them as I always was?

Yeah, right. Do I look crazy to you?

I didn't think so. And while I'm keeping it one-hundred, I'm really not as scared of them as I once was. I don't even sweat it, really. They're just a bunch of regular kids, just like I am. I mean, they may have a few rough edges, but we're really not all that different.

THE ADVENTURE CONTINUES